UP THE ANTE

Visit us at www.boldstrokesbooks.com

By the Author

From This Moment On

True Confessions

Missing

Trusting Tomorrow

Desperate Measures

Up the Ante

UP THE ANTE

by

PJ Trebelhorn

2015

UP THE ANTE

ISBN 13: 978-1-62639-237-3

This Trade Paperback Original Is Published By
Bold Strokes Books, Inc.
P.O. Box 249
Valley Falls, NY 12185

First Edition: January 2015

CREDITS
EDITOR: CINDY CRESAP
PRODUCTION DESIGN: SUSAN RAMUNDO
COVER DESIGN BY SHERI (GRAPHICARTIST2020@HOTMAIL.COM)

Acknowledgments

First and foremost, I want to thank Len Barot and everyone at Bold Strokes Books. I'm thankful every day to be a member of this amazing family.

Sheri, thank you for another wonderful cover.

My editor, Cindy Cresap, you make my words so much better, and I can't thank you enough.

There are only approximately 400,000 people worldwide who have multiple sclerosis. I've been lucky in that I haven't had many relapses of the disease since I was diagnosed in 2005.

I really thought that in the nine years since, I'd dealt with the emotional turmoil my diagnosis brought on, but found through writing Jordan's story, I'd suppressed a lot of those emotions. This book was more difficult to write than I thought it would be, and I just hope I did okay with it.

A huge thank you has to go to you, the readers. Your e-mails and encouraging words mean more than you could ever know. And it's because of you that all of us keep writing.

Dedication

For Cheryl, always

CHAPTER ONE

Jordan Stryker walked out of the nursing home, or assisted living facility as Matt preferred to call it, where her mother resided and took a seat on one of the benches in the courtyard. She looked west toward the ever-reddening sky and found herself wondering how they'd gotten to this point in their lives. Her father died from a self-inflicted gunshot wound seven years ago, when Jordan was thirty-six. Her brother, Matt, who was still inside trying to get their mother to remember something—anything—that happened more than five minutes earlier, had only been twenty-nine at the time.

Then there was their mother. Jordan knew for most families, the mother was the glue that held everything together. Not so for the Stryker clan. Most people who didn't know them assumed Evelyn was this way because she'd been sitting next to her husband on the couch when he put the muzzle of a gun in his mouth and pulled the trigger, resulting in blood and brain matter being splattered not only all over the wall behind him, but all over his wife as well.

It would have been enough to drive anyone mad, but Jordan knew her mother had been barreling toward this outcome for years. Maybe her husband's suicide had been the catalyst for her downfall, but there was no doubt in Jordan's mind she would have ended up in the same place eventually.

Jordan knew now that her childhood had been atypical, but at the time she hadn't known any better. She leaned forward and rested her head in her hands with a sigh.

Evelyn had been only sixteen when she'd found herself pregnant, and Jordan's father, Carl, was only a year older. Her mother's family was ashamed of the scandal, but since Carl had been drafted and was being sent off to Vietnam, they thought they'd have time to talk her out of marrying him when he returned home after his tour. Their plan didn't work though, and the two were married three months after Jordan was born.

As far as Jordan could tell, they'd never really been happy with each other. Hell, they weren't ever happy apart from each other either. She wasn't even entirely sure her father had been capable of being happy. Carl wasn't one to ever let an opportunity go by to tell Jordan he resented the fact he was forced into marrying. He blamed Jordan for all his problems in life, and he was convinced Evelyn had gotten pregnant on purpose in order to trap him. He even voiced his doubts Jordan was even his. He'd told her he wasn't cut out to be a father, and Jordan could certainly attest to that.

"Mind if I join you, or is this an invitation-only pity party?"

Jordan looked up at her younger brother and scooted over so he could sit. He handed her the cane she'd left inside. She studied his face for a moment as he gazed off in the distance. If it weren't for the seven-year age difference, they could have been twins. Their dark hair, green eyes, and model-like facial features hadn't come from either of their parents.

Their father had wanted both of them to follow in his footsteps and join the Marines. Jordan despised the idea so much she'd seriously considered joining the Navy out of spite. He'd been pissed when she announced her plans to join the

FBI. In his mind, defending the country against enemy forces was more noble and infinitely more important than catching criminals. She'd really thought it might kill him when Matt announced his intention of joining the FBI like his big sister instead of becoming a Marine.

"Have you told Mom you left the bureau?" he asked after a moment. "Or even that you were diagnosed with multiple sclerosis?"

"Why? What would be the point?" Jordan shook her head in frustration. They had this argument every time they discussed anything having to do with their mother. "She'd just forget it five minutes later, and even if she didn't, she wouldn't care."

"That's not true."

"The hell it isn't." Jordan fought to keep her emotions under control. She'd learned a long time ago anger got her nowhere with Matt when they were talking about their mother. As far as he was concerned, Evelyn was perfect. And perhaps she was, for him. She'd always treated him better. Maybe life growing up would have been more bearable if Jordan had been born a boy. She closed her eyes and took a deep breath in through her nose. "You know what? I'm not going to argue with you about this anymore. You go right on living in your little fantasy world where dementia is a curable disease. I'm done with it. I don't know why we continue to do this every single year."

"We do it because she's our mother, Jordan."

"Jesus, Matt, it really is that simple for you, isn't it?"

"Yes, it is," he said quietly. "It's her birthday."

Jordan could see the indignation in his eyes, and her heart broke a little for him. She wanted to feel the same way, but she just couldn't. She blamed her parents for shaping her into what she'd become—a woman incapable of maintaining a loving relationship. When you grow up with parents who did nothing but argue and fight constantly when they were together, that was what relationships were, and who wanted that? She set her cane against the end of the bench and turned to look at him.

"You're right. It is her birthday. But she doesn't know that, Matt. She doesn't even know who we are, for God's sake. She tells the staff here she has no family. If we never came back here again, she wouldn't even know the difference."

"I would. I'd know the difference," he said, pointing at his own chest to emphasize his argument. "I could never do that to her. Would you want your kids to ignore you?"

"Matty, I don't have kids. I'm forty-three years old, I'm single, I'm a lesbian, and I have MS. Chances are pretty good I won't *ever* have kids."

"Doesn't mean you couldn't meet some woman who already has one."

"I think you're forgetting the MS part. There are no relationships in my future."

"Have you ever even had a relationship?"

Jordan looked up at the darkening sky and tried not to think about Los Angeles. She tried not to think about Ashley Green. But a funny thing always happened when she consciously tried to not think about Ash—she ended up thinking of nothing *but* Ash. It was infuriating, but at least it didn't happen nearly as often now as it had in the past.

When she looked back at him, he was staring at her, waiting patiently for her response. She simply shook her head.

"I don't believe you," he said with a slow smile. "You went somewhere just now. You checked out. What's her name?"

"It doesn't matter. I haven't seen or spoken to her in fifteen years. And to be perfectly honest, if I ran into her tomorrow,

I'd probably turn right around and walk away. Hell, I doubt I'd even recognize her."

"She broke your heart, didn't she?"

Jordan had to laugh. She knew if she didn't she'd probably end up crying. She wasn't sure where the impeccable insight her brother possessed came from, because it sure wasn't a trait either of their parents passed along.

"Why didn't you ever tell me about her?"

"It wasn't one of my proudest moments, Matt. She was straight. She was married. They were trying to have a kid. I went into it with my eyes wide open, and I was stupid enough to let her get close enough to be able to break my heart. I've made damn sure to never make that mistake again."

"You had an affair with a married woman?" He sounded surprised, and she couldn't blame him. She always told him she would never even think about getting involved with a straight woman, married or not.

"No," she answered after a moment. "I had a *relationship* with a married woman. Unfortunately, she didn't see it the same way. To her it was nothing but a fling. When she was finished with me, she threw me out like I was no better than an empty ice cream carton. But I knew better than to fall for her, so it's my own damn fault. And it doesn't matter anyhow, because it was a lifetime ago. Or at least it feels that way."

They were both silent then, and Jordan found her mind wandering to Ash. She wondered what Ash was doing now. It was her birthday tomorrow, and why the hell should she remember that? Did they ever have the kid she'd wanted so badly? She shook her head. It wasn't doing her any good to stroll down memory lane. Especially not the particular lane leading to Ashley Green.

"You aren't leaving for Vegas until tomorrow, right?" Matt asked, obviously knowing she was ready for a change in the subject.

"Right. Tomorrow afternoon."

"Will you have dinner with me tonight?"

"Absolutely." Jordan smiled sadly at him as he stood and looked over his shoulder at the building.

"I'm going back in for a minute. I'll be knocking on your hotel room door in about forty-five minutes, so be ready."

"I will be."

Matt walked away and Jordan could see the defeat in his posture. He knew the things she said about their mother were true, but he'd always been one to look at the sunny side of everything. When he was a kid his optimism had always left him disappointed. Now, as an adult, it was apparently having the same outcome.

Jordan closed her eyes and listened to the sound of the crickets all around her. She'd always done her best to keep Matt from getting hurt, but it was inevitable growing up with an alcoholic mother and an overbearing career Marine for a father. It seemed neither of them could ever do anything to please their parents. It didn't stop them from trying though, but disillusionment waited around every corner. As Matt got older things got easier for him, but Jordan hadn't been so lucky.

She remembered their mother's thirty-third birthday when Jordan was sixteen, and Matt was nine. Their father had been out of town for one thing or another, and Matt had wanted to surprise their mother with a party just for the three of them. Jordan tried to talk him out of it, but he had his mind set. They decorated the house and made a cake. Jordan even made dinner, but she knew their mother wouldn't make it home. She rarely did when her husband was out of town. They waited at the dinner table for almost two hours before finally going to the living room to watch television. At ten, she sent Matt to bed and she waited in the dark for their mother to come home.

It was after midnight when she finally stumbled through the front door. Jordan was about to confront her when she realized she wasn't alone. There was a man with her, and based on where his hands were, Jordan was pretty sure the guy was more than just a friend. She shrank back into the couch and prayed they wouldn't come into the living room.

She heard her mother laughing quietly as the guy's hands covered her breasts, and Jordan had closed her eyes. She really didn't want to witness her mother being unfaithful. It was bad enough to know she was, and even worse she had to hear it, but there was no way she was going to watch it as well. She heard her mother whisper they needed to be quiet because she didn't want to wake up the kids. The man said something Jordan couldn't make out, but then her mother moaned loudly. She told him he could stay, but he had to be gone before the kids got up for school in the morning. Then Jordan heard them going up the stairs to the bedroom.

A car door slamming in the parking lot brought her back to the present. She shook her head to get rid of any lingering thoughts and grabbed her cane before standing. She'd never told anyone about that night, nor the subsequent nights their mother either brought home a man or simply never came home. As far as she knew, Matt had no idea she'd ever been unfaithful. Jordan vowed a long time ago to make sure he never found out.

Chapter Two

Ashley Noble woke with the sun in her eyes. She turned onto her side in an attempt to go back to sleep, but there was a warm body next to her. She stiffened slightly as an arm went around her waist and the woman she was in bed with groaned softly in her sleep. Ash held her breath and mentally counted to ten before carefully extricating herself from the other woman's grasp.

She picked up her clothes from the floor as she headed for the bathroom. Once there, she shut the door and breathed a sigh of relief. She really needed to stop this. Waking up in random women's hotel rooms was getting old. She splashed cold water on her face and looked at her reflection in the mirror.

"You don't look like you're forty years old," she said quietly, turning her head slightly so she could study the crow's feet around her eyes. "All right, maybe you do. But you look pretty damn good for being the age you once thought was ancient."

She dug her cell phone out of her pocket to check the time. Six thirty. In the morning. She sighed and ran a hand through her hair. Too damn early considering she didn't have to be to work until three in the afternoon. She quickly dressed before opening the door slowly so she could peek and make sure the woman was still asleep. There was a reason she only hooked up with tourists—she never had to see them again. And she was *always* gone before they woke up in the morning.

And she never picked up anyone in *her* casino. Too much of a risk of running into them again, and that would never end well. And the Rio was far enough from the strip that they didn't get too many people just wandering in to throw their money away. Chances were, if someone was in the casino of the Rio, they were staying at the hotel too. So she'd made the decision early on that she'd stay far away from the women in her casino.

She closed the door behind her and hurried down the hallway to the elevator that would take her to the hotel lobby and casino floor. She made a beeline for the parking garage in case anyone she knew saw her. Vegas wasn't really that small, but she knew a lot of people who lived and worked there. Within five minutes, she was exiting the garage and heading home.

"Happy birthday," she said to her reflection in the rearview mirror. She always thought she'd be settled down by the time she hit forty. Not that she hadn't tried. Hell, fifteen years ago she'd been married and attempting to start a family. Then Jordan Stryker walked into her life, and Ashley was never the same.

Until the day she met Jordan, Ash always assumed she was straight because it was all she'd ever known. Sure, she'd been attracted to girls, but she thought that was normal for a teenager. She'd been Homecoming Queen, dated the star of the high school football team, and even married him right after graduation. To this day, she couldn't believe she was with him for eighteen years, considering they'd first started dating in junior high school. She'd somehow managed to convince herself she was happy, but until Jordan, Ash hadn't known what happy truly was. And then she *still* hadn't left her husband until almost nine years later.

"Fuck," she mumbled. She hadn't thought about Jordan in years. Not much, anyway. She couldn't deny the reason she'd never been able to make a relationship with a woman last. She'd tried a couple of times right after she came out, but inevitably she would always compare them to Jordan. She hadn't wanted to, but she couldn't help it.

When she pulled into her garage, it was just after seven. She walked in and glanced at the answering machine long enough to determine there were no messages. Not a surprise since she hardly gave out her home number any longer. It was time to seriously think about getting rid of the landline and going strictly with the cell. In fact, the only reason she still had the house phone was because it was the only number her parents had for her.

She'd known there wouldn't be a message from them wishing her a happy birthday, but knowing it didn't stop her from hoping. Some people might say, "It's early, they might still call." But Ash knew better. They were retired, but they still woke with the sun every morning, her dad going to play golf with his buddies on most days, and her mom puttering around the garden or meeting with her book club.

No, they wouldn't call. She hadn't spoken to either of them since she'd left Los Angeles. At first, she'd hoped they would come around eventually, but who could blame them for being confused as hell when their only daughter ended a thirteen-year marriage because she suddenly decided she was a lesbian? Of course it hadn't really happened that way, but it was how they saw it since it seemingly came out of the blue. So for the past six years there were no phone calls or cards on birthdays and holidays. Ash tried hard not to let it bother

her, but she'd always been so close to both her parents, it was difficult not to let it get to her sometimes.

She poured herself a glass of orange juice and took a seat at the kitchen table just as Trixie, her tuxedo cat, jumped onto the table and made her displeasure known by flicking her tail in Ash's face.

"I know, you hate it when I stay out all night," Ash said, wiping the fur from her face. "I'm sure you used to do the same thing before I gave you a home though, so you don't have any right to judge me, baby girl."

Trixie sat and looked at her with the attitude only a cat could have. She blinked slowly and looked away, almost as though she was telling Ash she couldn't care less. But Ash knew better. She loved this cat like she'd never loved another animal before. When she reached over to scratch under Trixie's chin, the cat leaned into her touch and closed her eyes as she began to purr loudly, any perceived snub wiped away in an instant.

Trixie jumped and backed away from her as she swatted at the cell phone vibrating on the table next to her. Ash laughed as she picked it up and saw it was Kelly Osgood, first shift supervisor of security at the Rio All-Suites Hotel and Casino.

"This better be important, Oz, because even Trixie isn't happy you're calling this early in the morning," she said by way of greeting.

"Tell Trixie it is indeed important. I wouldn't want that cat pissed at me," Oz replied, a hint of humor in his voice. "I know you can't wait for the World Series of Poker to be over and done with, but I was looking over the list of people registered to play in the no-limit hold 'em tournament starting this Sunday. I came across a name I was pretty sure might be of some interest to you."

"And it couldn't wait until I got there this afternoon?"

"Please, if I know you—and I'm pretty sure I do—you just walked in the door. So don't be acting all high and mighty and accusing me of waking you up with an early morning phone call." He paused then, no doubt waiting for her to respond, but she said nothing. "Of course, if I'm completely out in left field with my assumption, I apologize."

"Just tell me the name, Oz." There was no way Ash was going to give him the satisfaction of knowing he was right, so she made a concerted effort to give nothing away in her tone.

"Jordan Stryker. And she's staying at the hotel too."

Ash felt lightheaded and she gripped the edge of the table with her free hand. She was vaguely aware her heart rate had spiked dramatically, and she felt dangerously close to passing out. She mumbled something she hoped sounded like *I'll call you back* before disconnecting and dropping the phone back onto the table.

Shit. Jordan was in town? And staying at *her* hotel? What were the odds? In Vegas the odds were supposed to be in the house's favor, weren't they? Ash stood and began to pace, her hand raking through her hair as she began talking to herself. Trixie watched her as though she might dart from the room at any second.

"I'll just have to do my best to avoid her," she said to herself but she was looking at Trixie. "She's here to play poker, so I just need to stay away from the poker room. I can avoid her for a few days, right? Of course the series is going on for more than two weeks, but she can't possibly be here for the entire thing, can she? Piece of cake."

She took a deep breath as she sat again, feeling more like herself after walking it off and talking it out. Trixie was still watching her warily but stood her ground. Ash picked up the phone and called Oz back.

"Are you all right, Ash?" he asked when he answered. "Should I not have told you?"

"I'm fine, and of course you should have told me. Much preferable to running into her completely unaware. When does she check-in and out?"

"Check-in is this evening and it's an open reservation. She didn't give a check-out date. You sure you're okay?"

"Yeah." Ash laughed in an attempt to convince him her world hadn't just been turned upside down. "Could you do me a favor?"

"Name it."

"Change the schedule for this evening. I want someone else in the poker areas tonight, whether just regular poker or the WSOP area. I want to stay strictly in the slots area tonight."

"You got it. I'll see you later?"

"Of course you will." She hung up abruptly and shoved the phone into her pocket before rinsing out her glass and going upstairs for a shower. There was no way in hell she was going to be able to get back to sleep now.

CHAPTER THREE

Jordan exited the elevator into the main lobby of the Rio All-Suites Hotel and Casino in Las Vegas at almost six that evening. She shook her head in wonder at the opulence on display. It was beyond her how people could walk into a casino, see the amount of money on exhibit in the garish décor, and still think they had any chance in hell of striking it rich. Where did those people think the owners got the money to constantly make upgrades to their hotels and casinos?

The young man who'd taken her bags out of her trunk at the front entrance waved to her from the check-in desk. She waved back and concentrated on getting across the space without limping. She'd managed to convince herself she wouldn't need her cane, which was with her luggage, which in turn was by the check-in desk. She should have known almost five hours in the car and the desert heat would wreak havoc with her multiple sclerosis.

She forced a smile at the woman who checked her in, even though she wanted nothing more than a place to sit down and relax for the next month. She got the security card that would allow her entrance to her room and then followed her luggage.

"Is this your first time in Vegas?" the young man asked.

"No," Jordan said as she glanced at his name tag. "I've been here quite a few times, Mark."

"Business or pleasure?"

"A little of both in the past, but this time, purely pleasure." Jordan leaned against the back of the elevator and closed her eyes momentarily.

"Are you all right, Ms. Stryker?"

"Fine," she answered quickly. She hated showing weakness, especially to strangers. For some reason, strangers always thought you needed help if they perceived weakness. Especially men. Mark didn't seem like the type though. If she had to guess, she'd say Mark was family. There wasn't really anything in particular in his appearance or demeanor to bring her to that conclusion, but it was just a feeling she had. She looked at him and smiled. "Just tired is all."

"Okay," he said as the elevator doors opened onto her floor. She motioned for him to go ahead. He knew where they were going better than she did. He kept talking away as they went down the hall. "We have pretty much everything here in the hotel you could possibly need, but if you want suggestions on where to go for anything else, don't hesitate to ask for me."

They stopped at her door and he slid the card through the reader. When it clicked and the green light flashed, he pushed down on the handle and opened the door. She went in ahead of him and walked straight to the floor-to-ceiling windows that looked out at the view of the strip, hoping her mouth wasn't hanging open in awe. She was sure it would be even more impressive after dark.

"You can just leave the bags at the foot of the bed," she told him without turning around. She listened as he unloaded the cart.

"All the phone numbers you need are on a list here by the phone. Is there anything else I can do for you right now?"

Jordan reached into her pocket and pulled out a twenty-dollar bill before walking to him and placing it in his palm. He handed her a card with his name and phone number on it and gave her a wink as he leaned closer.

"That's my cell phone number. If you find you want to go out and meet other women, give me a call. I know the best places to go. Unfortunately, there aren't any bars here in the hotel for family to congregate."

"I didn't think I was that obvious," Jordan said with a laugh she couldn't contain.

"I'm sure you wouldn't be to a straight man, but you pinged my gaydar the second you pulled up to the entrance." He straightened his posture and was all business once again. "I hope you enjoy your stay at the Rio All-Suites Hotel and Casino, Ms. Stryker. If you need anything, please don't hesitate to call the front desk and ask for me."

With that, he was gone, and Jordan placed his card on the bedside table before grabbing the television remote and sitting on the couch to relax for a while before heading out to dinner. It was Wednesday evening, and her first tournament didn't start until noon Sunday. She planned on spending her time between now and then doing nothing but hanging out by the pool and enjoying herself.

❖

Jordan woke an hour later when her cell phone began vibrating in her pocket. She pulled it out and sighed when she saw her mother's name displayed. She was supposed to call her when she arrived to let her know she'd gotten to Vegas in one piece. She sat up, wincing slightly at the pain in her right leg, and answered the call. Honestly, she'd assumed her mother had forgotten all about her visit, much less the promise to call her.

"Hi, Mom," she said, trying not to sound like she'd been asleep.

"I was worried about you. You said you'd call when you got there."

Jordan rolled her eyes and ran her fingers through her hair. She couldn't remember a time her mother had been genuinely worried about anything other than herself. Something Matt said at dinner the previous night went through her mind.

"No matter how we were treated while we were growing up, she's still our mother. She's sick, and she needs us to take care of her now."

Jordan sighed and looked out at the view of the strip. The sun was going down and most of the lights were starting to hint at the grandeur to come when it was fully dark. Jordan knew she should just be grateful their mother was living in the nursing home near Flagstaff. At least the "taking care of her" part wasn't a full-time, hands-on endeavor for either her or Matt.

"Sorry, Mom. Traffic was hellacious, and checking into the hotel took forever. I just got to my room and was about to call you." Jordan was surprised at how easily the lies came.

"Just as long as you made it there okay," her mother said. "Good luck with your game tomorrow, dear."

"It's Sunday."

"What?"

"My first tournament. It starts Sunday."

"Oh, right. You'll call tomorrow night and let me know how you did, right?"

"Sure, Mom. I'll talk to you then." She hung on, waiting for her mother hang up first—a habit from when she was a teenager. The one time she'd hung up before her mother, she never heard the end of it because her mother hadn't been finished speaking to her.

She shoved the phone back into the pocket of her cargo shorts and rested her head against the back of the couch, her eyes closed. Her mother's memory had been steadily getting worse over the past decade. The doctors had diagnosed her with dementia, but they thought it could possibly be a result of her heavy drinking and drugs for more than thirty years. Those particular vices only got worse after Jordan's father committed suicide.

She shook her head to get rid of the memories she'd rather not think about. It was bad enough her parents had ruined her childhood. She wasn't about to let them ruin her life now.

She grabbed five hundred dollar bills from her suitcase and shoved them in her pocket. A few hours at a poker table would give her something else to concentrate on, but first she needed food. Mark had been right about one thing—there were enough restaurants and shops inside the hotel, she'd probably never have to leave for anything. Unless she decided she wanted some female companionship. She made sure she had his card in her wallet just in case.

She walked to the door of her room and back to the windows to be certain she could get by without her cane and then snatched the key card from the dresser before heading for the elevator.

Chapter Four

After a quick burger at one of the many casual dining establishments on the main floor of the casino, Jordan put her name on the waiting list for an open seat at a poker table. She got lucky and only had to wait for about thirty minutes. Hopefully, it was a sign of good things to come on this trip.

An hour later, she was finding her groove and was up almost a thousand dollars. Jordan didn't like chatter while she was playing, but she seemed to be at a table full of talkers. She did her best to tune them all out, but it was no use. Whether she wanted to or not, she knew all their names, if they had kids and/or grandkids, and where they were all from. It seemed the only thing they didn't supply were medical records.

She spared a quick glance at her cards but gave no outward sign of what she had. Pocket aces. She was always careful to not change her expression no matter how good or bad her starting hand was. Art, a grandfather of three from Tennessee a couple of seats from the small blind, went all in. The next two players, Jimmy and Tara, called his bet, as did Jordan. The remaining players folded.

The flop gave her another ace along with two kings. Her heart rate quickened, but she never took her gaze from Jimmy, the first to bet in the second round. She noticed sweat on his forehead. She was certain he had nothing by how hard he was thinking about whether to bet or check. He finally checked, and Tara, seated next to Jordan, pushed a hundred-dollar chip in.

Jordan hesitated for a few seconds and made a show of first counting her chips and then looking at her cards again. She knew there was only one hand she could lose to at this point, and that would be pocket kings. But if Tara had kings, she would have bet bigger based on how she'd played previous hands. There was always a chance Art, who'd gone all in before the flop, had kings, but she had to play her gut. After taking one more look at her cards, she pushed all her chips in. Jimmy folded, and Jordan could tell by the smile on her face Tara thought she had her beat. Jordan knew her hesitation was what made Tara feel that way. Tara pushed all her chips in and the three of them turned their cards over. Jordan stood behind her chair, her hands gripping the back of it tight enough for her knuckles to turn white.

Art had queens. Tara had ace-king. The odds were in her favor, but the other two still had a chance. The turn was a two—Art was done. As long as the river wasn't a king, she'd win. She closed her eyes for a moment and heard Tara chanting *king, king, king,* under her breath. Jordan opened her eyes as a six was revealed.

"Fuck," Tara said. She looked at Jordan and shook her head, but the smile told Jordan she wasn't really mad about losing the hand. "Well played."

"Thanks," Jordan said as she sat once again and raked in her chips. She motioned to the dealer she was ready to cash out and he gave her a tray for her winnings. When she was done stacking them she pushed a hundred dollar chip across the table, a tip for the dealer, and turned to leave, but Tara was still standing behind her.

"Can I buy you a drink?"

"I don't drink much," Jordan told her.

"How about coffee then?"

Jordan wanted to just go back to her room, but how could she say no to a beautiful woman? She finally nodded her consent and they made their way to the cashier so she could turn her chips in. While she waited for the woman to count it all, she saw another woman in a tailored suit enter the caged area with the cashiers. She felt her heart stop. Or maybe it dropped. She never did understand those old clichés. She felt as though she might actually pass out and had to grip the edge of the counter to ensure she stayed on her feet. The woman turned and their eyes met briefly before they both looked away.

Ashley.

Jordan thought they'd never run into each other again, but apparently it really was a small world after all. She'd told Matt she probably wouldn't even recognize her, but there was no mistaking those deep blue eyes and the curves. And the blond hair that hung just past her shoulders.

All Jordan could hear was the pulse pounding in her ears. When she was finally able to look again, Ashley was walking away. Jordan watched as she walked out to the casino floor and then disappeared into the crowd without so much as another glance in her direction. When the woman on the other side of the glass was done counting out her money, Jordan looked at her.

"The woman who was just in there," she said, surprised her voice was steady. "Is her name Ashley Green?"

"No," she replied with a shake of her head. "Her name is Ashley Noble. She's head of security here."

Jordan nodded absently as she pocketed her winnings and turned to walk away. Noble? She wondered at the name change. Had Ashley and her husband split, and perhaps Ash remarried? Or maybe it was her maiden name. And why was a Los Angeles cop working as head of security for a casino in Las Vegas?

Jordan was halfway to the elevators that would have taken her to her room when she felt a hand on her forearm. She turned to find Tara, a concerned look on her face.

"I thought we were having a cup of coffee? Are you all right?"

"I'm fine." But not really, she thought. Fuck, one glimpse of Ash and she forgot what she was doing. They headed away from the elevators and toward the Starbucks. Ashley had completely derailed Jordan's life fifteen years ago, and it was obvious she still had the ability to do it now.

❖

Shit, shit, shit, Ashley thought as she walked at a brisk pace out of the cashier's area. She concentrated on her job and tried not to think about how affected she was by seeing Jordan again. Out of all the casinos in Las Vegas, why in the world did Jordan have to choose hers? They weren't even on the strip, for God's sake. She didn't stop walking until she made it back to her office. After closing the door, she went to sit behind her desk and worked on slowing down her breathing.

There was some gray in Jordan's dark brown hair, but otherwise she looked much the same as she had when they'd been in Los Angeles. She was still fit and trim, and still looked like she could have walked off the pages of a magazine. And those green eyes. Jesus, they were more intense than she remembered.

There was a knock on the door a fraction of a second before it opened and one of her employees stuck her head inside.

"Ash, there's a guy at the blackjack tables who isn't very happy he lost all his money," Janine Price said. "He's being rather vocal about it. I know how much you like throwing people out, so…"

"Send Lars," Ash told her without any hesitation. Jan looked at her like she was crazy but just nodded once and disappeared again.

Her head was spinning. She'd seriously thought she would never see Jordan again. When Oz called her that morning, she vowed she'd do everything she could to avoid running into her. What she couldn't avoid was doing her job. She couldn't deny there was a part of her that was thrilled to know they were in the same building. She'd never been happy with the way they'd parted fifteen years ago.

Without thinking too much about what she was doing, she accessed the database that listed all the guests and their room numbers. She wasn't sure what she was going to do with the information she'd told Oz she didn't want. She quickly scribbled down the room number and closed the program on her computer. She stuffed the piece of paper in her suit jacket pocket just as her door opened again.

"Lars is on his way to deal with the belligerent customer," Jan said as she took a seat across the desk from her. "You want to tell me what's bothering you?"

Ashley leaned back in her chair and studied her face. Jan had been the first person she met when she'd moved to Vegas what seemed like a lifetime ago. She'd helped her to get a job at the Mirage and seemed to take it upon herself to take care of her. When Ash had been offered her current position as head of security at the Rio, she'd brought Jan and Oz both with her from the Mirage. They'd grown close over the years, and Jan and Oz were the only people she'd confided in about her reasons for leaving Los Angeles.

"Jordan is here," Ash finally said, trying her damnedest to sound as though it didn't affect her one way or the other.

"Jordan?" Jan asked, leaning forward and looking very interested. "*The* Jordan? What do you mean she's *here*?"

"She's here, in this casino."

"Have you talked to her? What did she say?"

"I didn't speak to her. We saw each other and I walked away." Ash ran a hand through her hair and looked at the ceiling. "Christ, Jan, I don't even know what I'd say to her if we did talk."

"Has she changed? It's been a long time. She's probably overweight and lost her looks, right?"

Ash had to laugh. Jan was trying so hard to make her feel better about running into Jordan again, but her assessment was way off.

"No, she looks like she hasn't aged much at all, if you want to know the truth." Her body's reaction to seeing her embarrassed Ash, but she wasn't about to tell Jan she'd been instantly aroused. "She looks really good."

"I think that might be a good place to start a conversation."

"What?" Ash was indignant. It would definitely *not* be a good place to start a conversation. Not after the way things ended. So much had changed, and she wasn't even sure now Jordan would be willing to talk to her. "No."

"Ash—"

"I said no, Jan." She stood and avoided looking at her. She knew Jan was attracted to her—it was something Jan admitted to her one night when they ran into each other in a local bar. But Ash's rule of not getting involved with anyone who actually lived in Vegas wasn't something she was going to break, especially for someone she worked with. It wasn't that Jan wasn't attractive. Hell, she was gorgeous, but Ash knew it could only lead to trouble. She didn't want to risk losing their friendship. "It's time to get back to work. She can't be here forever, so I just need to keep my eyes open and steer clear of her until she's gone."

"Keep telling yourself that, Ash. Maybe you can fool yourself into believing it." Jan left without another word and Ash fell back into her chair.

Jan could be a bit of a flake sometimes, but she'd always been a good friend. Her personal life was more than a little suspect since she played the field even more than Ash did, and Jan didn't care if the women she hooked up with lived in Vegas, or even if they were staying at the Rio. It had made for a couple of interesting encounters when a woman Jan had dumped confronted her on the floor, but Ash had bailed her out more than once. She wasn't sure how much longer she could do it though.

And if Jan were to set her sights on Jordan, well, Ash didn't know what she'd do. All she knew for sure was the jealousy that gripped her at the mere thought of Jan's hands on Jordan scared the crap out of her. She'd never been jealous before. But then again, Jordan always had made her feel things she wasn't used to feeling.

Chapter Five

This was a really bad idea. Jordan's head knew it, but her body seemed to be having other ideas. Tara made no bones about what she wanted from her. The frequent touches on Jordan's arm and the way she'd lean into her while they were talking made it obvious. Maybe she could feign a headache. No, not until after they'd gotten their coffee, because that would just be rude, wouldn't it? Jordan ordered, but when Tara reached into her pocket to get money, she stopped her.

"No, I've got it," Jordan said.

"I invited you for coffee," Tara reminded her.

"It's the least I can do since I took all your money at the poker table."

"Well, since you put it that way…" Tara smiled and ran a hand down Jordan's back.

When the barista gave her their cups, they made their way to a small table in the corner. Jordan sat and automatically added cream and sugar to hers as her mind wandered. She'd managed to not think about Ash for months now until she'd told Matt about her the day before. And now she couldn't believe she'd run into her again. How could it be at all possible for the mere sight of Ash to affect her like this?

"So, are you here alone?" Tara asked, pulling Jordan back from her introspective moment.

"Yes, I am. You?"

"I'm here with my sister. I'm sure she's found some man to hang out with by now. We've been in town for a whole six hours." Tara took a sip of her coffee but held Jordan's gaze. "How long are you here for?"

"I'm not sure. I'm registered for a couple of tournaments, but I wanted to see how I did before deciding whether to register for the Main Event."

"The Main Event?"

"The World Series of Poker," Jordan said. "That's why I'm here."

"Then you're a pro? No wonder you cleaned us all out."

"Not hardly." Jordan chuckled and took a moment to think how odd it was to be having a normal conversation with someone who wasn't Ash when all she could think about was Ash. "I've only been playing for a few years but wanted to give it a try."

"Maybe we could go up to your room and you could show me how good you are." Tara reached across the table and covered her hand. Jordan allowed the touch for a second before slowly pulling her hand away.

"We aren't talking about poker anymore, are we?" Jordan asked as Tara shook her head. "I'm flattered, but I can't."

"God, please don't tell me you're straight."

"Definitely not."

"Then you have a girlfriend?"

"No."

"So what's the problem?"

Jordan took a deep breath. What was the problem? Tara was attractive enough, and she'd never had a problem with one-nighters in the past. In fact, since being diagnosed, it was all she'd been interested in. She didn't want to examine the reason too closely because she knew the answer—Ash.

But Ash didn't want her. She'd made that perfectly clear the last time they'd seen each other. Maybe Ash didn't want her, but Tara clearly did, so why not? *Just go with it,* a voice in her head said.

"What about your sister?"

"She won't care. Like I said, she's probably found a guy to hang with."

Jordan ignored the part of her brain consumed with Ash and stood. She motioned for Tara to follow her and then headed toward the elevators again. If she could manage to keep Ash out of her thoughts, she might just be able to salvage the night.

Ash walked out to the parking garage with Jan when their shift was over, but once Jan drove away she pulled the piece of paper out of her pocket and stared at the room number she'd written down.

What the fuck was she thinking? She wouldn't blame Jordan if she didn't want to talk to her. She should just do what she told Jan she was going to do. Avoid her at all costs, and she'd be gone again soon enough. She crumpled the paper and tossed it onto the floor before turning the key in the ignition.

She put the car in reverse and started to back out, but the car stalled. She sat there for a moment in stunned silence. Maybe it was a sign. The car was an automatic, for God's sake. It had never stalled before. She took a deep breath and pulled the key out, knowing it was inevitable. She had to talk to Jordan and explain her reasoning for ending their short-lived affair. It was something she'd wanted to do years ago, but she'd never had the guts to call her. She put her name tag into the glove box and got out before she could change her mind.

❖

It took Ash an unprecedented twenty minutes to make it to Jordan's door. She'd started to leave no less than four times before finally making it onto the elevator. Now that she was standing outside her room, she told herself how stupid this was. Her heart was racing with the anticipation of coming face-to-face with Jordan after so many years. How would Jordan react to seeing her again? Ash wouldn't blame her if Jordan didn't want to talk to her. Before she lost her nerve, she knocked and then took a step back from the door.

"Can you get that for me?" she heard Jordan say from inside.

Shit, she isn't alone.

But of course she wouldn't be alone. Ash was sure there wasn't any length of time in the past fifteen years Jordan would have been alone. She convinced herself to run away just as the door opened. A rather attractive woman with short dark hair was smiling at her.

"Can I help you?" she asked.

"I'm looking for Jordan," Ash said, thankful the woman was fully dressed.

"Who is it?" Jordan asked as she came out of the bathroom and stopped dead in her tracks when their eyes met. "Ash."

"Stryker," Ash said, using the name she'd gone by when they were working together. She felt as if she might pass out. She felt a smile trying to form on her lips and silently cursed herself. She didn't look away from Jordan, but could see the other woman looking back and forth between the two of them in her peripheral vision. "I wanted to talk to you, but I can see you're busy. I'll catch up with you later."

She turned and hurried back down the hallway but stopped when she heard Jordan's voice.

"Ash, wait."

She looked back at her and did as she asked. She waited. Jordan said something to the woman in her room, but Ash was far enough away she couldn't hear. The woman looked less than happy as she disappeared back into the room to presumably get her purse and then walked quickly past Ash, bumping into her as she did. Ash slowly walked toward Jordan, who was still standing in the doorway.

"You didn't have to make your girlfriend leave." Ash stopped outside the door.

"Not my girlfriend. I just met her." Jordan appeared flustered, and Ash experienced an uncharacteristic bout of satisfaction to know she wasn't the only one affected by their meeting again. "Please, come in."

Ash hesitated for only a second. Jordan moved aside to allow her access. She walked past her and went right to the sofa, sitting without being invited to. She put her hands under her thighs so Jordan wouldn't see how badly they were trembling.

"So how did you find me, Ashley Noble?"

Ash whipped her head up and looked at her. She'd never told Jordan her maiden name, so how had she found out? Her emotions warred inside her. She was perturbed Jordan knew her maiden name and she wanted to confront her on it, but when she saw Jordan wince as she sat on the other end of the sofa, she worried about what would make her do so. She scanned the room and noticed a cane against the wall next to the bed.

"You're hurt." Not a question. It was obvious to Ash that Jordan was in pain. "What happened? Were you shot?"

"No," Jordan said without looking at her. "And don't think you can deflect my question. How did you find out what room I was in?"

"I'm head of security for the hotel. It wasn't really very hard to find the information."

"Then I'm guessing it probably wouldn't be good for anyone to find out you used your position to obtain a guest's room number, am I right?"

"Obviously, this was a mistake." Ash stood and walked toward the door. What the hell had she been thinking, showing up at Jordan's room? "I won't bother you again."

"Ash, wait." Jordan struggled to stand but managed to do it before Ash turned around. "I'm sorry. When I'm nervous I tend to be an ass."

"Just when you're nervous?"

Jordan couldn't help but laugh. Ash was right. She managed to be an ass most of the time. A trait she blamed solely on her father because he had perfected the art of being an ass. She could see Ash fighting not to smile, but at least she was walking back to the sofa. They sat again, and Jordan could tell Ash was nervous too. She wondered what it had cost her emotionally to show up at her room. She sent a silent thank you to whoever might be listening that she and Tara hadn't been in the middle of something.

"Why are you here?" Jordan asked.

"How did you know my last name?"

"Why are you head of security at a Las Vegas hotel? What happened to your career as a police officer?"

"Why are you trying to hide the fact you're in pain?"

Jordan sat back and looked at the ceiling. Rapid-fire questions were getting them nowhere. There was no way she was going to tell Ash about her MS. She'd wanted many things from Ash, but sympathy had never been one of them.

"How about we try answering some of the questions we've already asked instead of adding more to the mix?"

"Fine. How did you know my last name?"

"I'm a former FBI agent. I have my ways of finding things like that out."

"*Former* FBI agent?" Ash's expression and tone told Jordan she should have kept her mouth shut. "What the hell's going on, Stryker?"

"I love it when you say my name like that."

"Damn it, Jordan, I'm serious."

"So am I," Jordan said. When she'd left Flagstaff that afternoon she'd never dreamed she'd be sitting in her hotel room talking to Ashley Green. *No, it's Noble now.* She couldn't help herself around Ash—flirting seemed to be the normal thing to do.

"You're obviously in pain," Ash said. Jordan wasn't sure if she was relieved or not that Ash wasn't going to be easily deterred from her line of questioning. "And you're a *former* FBI agent. Not retired. Were you shot?"

"No, and you already asked that question. I just have some muscle spasms in my leg." It wasn't a total lie. It just wasn't the complete truth either. Jordan didn't feel comfortable revealing her medical situation to anyone, much less Ash. Certainly not at this stage of the game anyway, and quite possibly never. "And as far as the job? I was getting burned out. I decided I wanted to do other things."

"Like gamble? Is that really smart?"

"Trust me, when I play cards, it isn't gambling," Jordan said with a cocky grin.

"If I find out you're counting cards, I'll throw you out so fast your head will spin."

"Relax. I play poker. And if I could count cards, I'd have a hell of a lot more money than I do, I can tell you that. I'm here to play in the World Series."

"You're that good?"

"Do you have to ask?"

"Jesus, you haven't changed at all, have you?" Ash asked. She sounded annoyed, but Jordan could tell she was once again trying not to smile.

"Nope, not a bit." *Especially not where you're concerned.* "You didn't seem to mind it the first time we met."

"That was a long time ago."

"It was," Jordan agreed. "But here we are, fifteen years later, and you're obviously not with your husband anymore. So apparently you've changed quite a bit."

"I have."

"You haven't told me why you're here in my room."

Jordan waited while Ash seemed to be struggling with what to say in response. In Jordan's experience, the long pause was simply to allow the other person to sort the lie out in their head before speaking.

"I feel like I owe you an apology for how things ended between us."

Jordan was a little surprised. She'd been crushed when it happened, but she never expected Ash to apologize for it. She'd known when they started that Ash was married. She and her husband had been trying to have a baby, for God's sake. She'd never been expecting anything to come of their affair, but to be told in no uncertain terms that Ash never wanted to see or hear from her again kind of bruised her ego to say the least.

"You don't have to apologize," Jordan said.

"Yes, I do. I hurt you, and I swear to you I never meant to do that." Ash looked down at her hands on her knees, and Jordan waited to see if there was more to come. After a couple of moments, Ash met her eyes again. "I thought it would be best for both of us to cut all ties. I was wrong."

"You could have called me."

"You could have called me too."

"You made me promise not to," Jordan reminded her. Ash turned away from her, but not before Jordan saw the sad smile. "How long have you been divorced?"

"Six years. It took me that long to realize I'd never really been in love with him. How sad is that?"

"At least you finally did realize it. Some people stay in their marriage forever and never even consider there might be something they're missing." Jordan thought of her parents and how they'd stayed together at all costs, neither of them ever even mentioning the word divorce. She did her best to stand without giving away how much pain she was in. She got a bottle of water from the mini fridge and held it up. "Can I get you something to drink? I have water, soda, or I think there's enough alcohol in this thing for ten people to get drunk on."

"I'm fine," Ash replied without looking at her. Her focus was on the Vegas strip and all the lights flashing. Jordan couldn't blame her. It was an amazing sight to see. It almost looked bright enough to be the middle of the day.

"So, I'm assuming you have a boyfriend?"

"Why would you think that?"

"I can't imagine you alone is all." Jordan took her seat again and took a drink from her bottle. "Any man would be lucky to have you."

"I'm gay."

Jordan felt like the wind had been knocked out of her. When they'd been together, Ash insisted she wasn't a lesbian. Jordan had taken her at her word. She'd appeared to be happy in her marriage. Ashley and Kevin were going to have a family, and they were going to grow old together. *That* was the reality she'd convinced herself of over the years. Now she was finding out she'd been wrong.

"Say something," Ash said after a few moments.

"What would you like me to say?" Jordan asked, trying to keep any emotion out of her voice. She was torn between being angry at having been lied to, and being hopeful at the possibility of something happening between them again. But no, that would never happen. At least nothing long-term. Her multiple sclerosis prevented long-term with anyone. "You cheated me out of my toaster oven."

Ash laughed, and Jordan found herself filled with joy at the sound. God, she'd missed her. Having her there in the same room, on the same couch, filled a void in Jordan's heart she hadn't even realized was there.

"You're still beautiful when you laugh," Jordan told her, but regretted it almost immediately when Ash turned serious again.

"I should go."

"Ash, wait." She reached out and gently touched her forearm. "I'm sorry. I can't help but speak the truth."

"It's okay," Ash said with what was clearly a forced smile. "I need to get home."

"Oh," Jordan said, her heart sinking at the nuance of Ash's words.

"What?"

"Your girlfriend isn't very understanding about you being in a hotel room with a former lover, I take it."

Ash snorted before she stood and looked down at Jordan. "Would you be?"

"No." Jordan felt her heart clench at what certainly sounded like an acknowledgment of a girlfriend waiting at home for Ash. She started to get to her feet again, but Ash placed a hand on her shoulder and shook her head.

"Don't get up. I'm pretty sure I can find my own way out."

"It was good to see you again, Ash."

"You too. But I'm sure we'll be running into each other since you're here for the World Series."

"Hey, Ash?" Jordan got to her feet and took a couple steps toward her.

"Yeah?" Ash looked hopeful as she turned to face her once again.

"Did you ever have the baby you were trying for?"

"No. No, I didn't." The hopeful look was replaced by a sadness that caused an ache in Jordan's chest.

"I'm sorry," Jordan said, taking a couple more steps in Ash's direction. The need to hold her was hard to ignore. Ash turned away, but Jordan stopped her. "One more thing."

"What, Stryker?" She turned back once more and looked frustrated. Jordan smiled because she could still annoy Ash. That had to count for something, right?

"Happy birthday," Jordan said. The smile she got in return was so painfully beautiful it almost melted Jordan's heart.

"Thank you, but how can you possibly remember when my birthday is?"

"Because it has to do with you. I remember everything about you."

Jordan felt rooted to her spot and was helpless to move, even if she'd wanted to. Ash closed the distance between them and didn't stop until she was mere inches away from her.

"You always were more perceptive than anyone I've known," Ash said before touching Jordan's cheek with the backs of her fingers. She shook her head and smiled.

"When I care about someone I make it a point to pay attention to the little things," Jordan said, her voice barely above a whisper. Ash moved her hand to the back of Jordan's neck and pulled her close enough so she could feel her breath on her lips. Jordan sucked in a breath and shook her head.

"Is this a bad idea?" Ash asked, her eyes focusing on Jordan's mouth.

"Yes, it is," Jordan said. She willed her body to move away, but it refused to listen. "I won't be the other woman again, Ash. I can't be."

Ash didn't move either, and Jordan felt light-headed as her blood rushed through her veins. After a few moments of staring into each other's eyes, Ash finally pressed her lips to Jordan's.

Jordan heard herself whimper and was embarrassed, but she put her hands on Ash's hips and pulled their bodies together. She tried to deepen the kiss, but as soon as her tongue caressed Ash's lips, Ash pulled back.

"Good-bye, Jordan," she said. "It was good to see you again."

She watched in stunned silence as Ash walked out the door. That certainly sounded like a final good-bye. Like a good-bye because I'll never see you again type of good-bye. When the door latched, she felt her heart breaking all over again.

CHAPTER SIX

Ash hurried down the hall toward the elevators, worrying that if she didn't, she'd end up going right back to Jordan's room. Back to her arms. God, it had felt good to kiss her again. But she wasn't even sure where it had all come from. It had to be because she remembered her birthday, something everyone else in her life seemed to forget this year. Seriously? They hadn't seen each other in fifteen years, and she's going to remember when her birthday is?

When the elevator arrived, she pushed the button for the casino floor and leaned against the back wall, her eyes closed. She knew she should have corrected Jordan's wrong assumption about a girlfriend waiting at home for her, but what would it have accomplished? It was better if she thought Ash was involved because there'd be no pressure should they run into each other again. Jordan looked good. There was no denying it. But it worried her she had a cane. Obviously, she didn't need it all the time, because she didn't have it earlier in the casino.

Muscle spasms, she'd said. Ash wasn't buying it. Granted, she didn't know much about muscle spasms, but she would have expected Jordan to tense when one hit. She didn't. She seemed to simply be in constant pain.

"It doesn't matter, Noble," she muttered under her breath. "It's not your problem."

But she couldn't help thinking it *was* her problem. She'd broken Jordan's heart before and she regretted it. Regretted it almost immediately, truth be told. She'd been scared to death when she realized she was falling in love with her. The only thing she could think to do was end things with her. The crushed look in Jordan's eyes that day haunted her for years afterward.

But Jordan had known all along Ash was married, and Ash told her up front she wasn't going to leave her husband. Was it her fault Jordan had fallen in love with her too?

If she could do it all over again, she would have left Kevin then instead of staying with him for nine more years. Letting Jordan go and staying with Kevin in a loveless marriage was the hardest thing Ashley had ever done. Yet at the same time, it was the easiest, because it was what everyone expected of her. She was supposed to be married and have kids. It was what her mother had drilled into her head since the day she was born. She'd never given so much as a thought to whether or not she might be gay. Not until Jordan came barreling into her life.

Jordan had awakened her to who she really was, and seeing her in the casino made her want to make things right between them. She knew they couldn't go back, but maybe they could at least be friends. She did her best to hold on to that thought as she drove herself home, knowing she wanted so much more than friendship from Jordan Stryker.

❖

Jordan picked up the phone and called Mark, even as she mentally kicked herself for not getting Tara's room number.

Winning at poker always turned her on, and she thought she was going to be able to scratch that itch with Tara. Ashley showing up kind of changed all that, but she was still feeling like she needed to let off some steam. After three rings, Mark answered.

"Hello?"

"Mark, it's Jordan Stryker in room fourteen twelve."

"Well, hello, Jordan Stryker. I didn't expect to hear from you so soon. I'm guessing you want to go out on the town?"

"Yeah," she said, her eyes closed. He gave her the name and address for a couple of different places and told her which one had the better lesbian clientele. When they hung up she took a quick shower and headed out, opting for a cab ride instead of trying to drive her car through town. Besides, if she decided to drink, she wouldn't want to drive anyway.

The music was loud and she could feel the bass deep in her chest even before walking into the club. She made her way to the bar and ordered a soda before turning and looking at the crowd. It was mostly men, but there were plenty of women as well. It was hard to tell if they were coupled up or single, so she decided to have a seat and observe for a bit. She was about to order another soda when she felt a hand on her shoulder.

"Would you like to dance?"

She smiled but shook her head and pointed to her cane. "Sorry, but I don't dance."

"Then do you mind if I sit here?"

"Be my guest." Jordan looked around the bar in an attempt not to look at the woman sitting next to her. She was stunning. When the woman placed a hand on her thigh, Jordan felt it between her legs. She turned her head to look at her.

"Most of the women here are so young," she said, leaning close to Jordan in order to be heard. "*Too* young."

Jordan nodded in response, not really knowing what to say, and not wanting to yell over the music. She noticed as she got older how the crowds in the bars got younger. It seemed a natural form of progression, yet this woman who looked to be at least Jordan's age sounded surprised at the revelation.

"Can I buy you a drink?"

"Ginger ale," Jordan said, raising her glass with a wry smile. The music stopped abruptly and a man with a microphone came on stage to announce the drag show beginning in a few minutes. Jordan turned toward the woman and held her hand out. "Jordan."

"Alyssa," she replied with a quick pump of her hand and a smile. "So, Jordan, if you don't drink, and you don't dance, what the hell are you doing in a dance club?"

"Atmosphere," she answered as she looked around the bar. "There's nothing like a gay bar if you want atmosphere."

"True," Alyssa agreed with a nod. She motioned for the bartender to bring them another round before leaning back against the bar and studying Jordan. Jordan fought not to squirm under the scrutiny. "You aren't a goody-two-shoes, are you?"

Jordan laughed a little too loudly, and she was aware of people looking at them since the music stopped and wasn't drowning out conversation any longer.

"Hardly. Just not a drinker." Jordan didn't tell her it was from fear of early onset dementia like her mother had. That particular fear wasn't something she'd ever revealed to anyone. Not even Matt. "Are you a tourist, or a local?"

"Tourist. I leave Saturday to return to Seattle. How about you?"

"Tourist," Jordan said. "I'm here from Philadelphia."

Jordan met her gaze and felt something unspoken pass between them. There was no worry about Alyssa wanting more than a good time, she was certain of it. Alyssa leaned closer to her with a grin.

"Your hotel or mine?"

Jordan started to decline the offer, but wasn't that her whole reason for being in the club in the first place? She downed her ginger ale and set the glass on the bar before standing with a smile of her own.

"Yours. I know it's got to be closer than mine since my hotel isn't even on the strip."

Chapter Seven

Jordan blinked her eyes and shook her head to clear away the cobwebs before sitting up and looking at the bedside clock. It was four in the morning. At best, she'd been out for two hours. She looked down at Alyssa sleeping soundly next to her, the sheet around her waist exposing her breasts. Jordan knew she should leave, but she couldn't resist. She placed a finger lightly on Alyssa's breast before moving it across her nipple.

Alyssa stirred in her sleep and moaned softly, her lips parted. Jordan leaned down and kissed her on the forehead before getting out of the bed and searching for her clothes.

"Don't go," Alyssa said quietly.

"I have to."

"Why?"

Why? Because she couldn't stop thinking about Ash. Jordan was sure that response wouldn't go over well. She pulled her underwear on and sat on the bed to pull on her socks.

"I just have to."

"You have a girlfriend back in Philly? So what? I have a girlfriend too, but you know what? She isn't here. You are. Please come back to bed. I'll feed you breakfast when we get up, and then we never have to see each other again."

Jordan shook her head and sighed. If she'd known Alyssa had a girlfriend she never would have come back to her room with her. Jordan tried to stand when she felt Alyssa moving behind her, but Alyssa's arms went around her waist and pulled her back against her body. She tried to ignore the growing arousal when Alyssa's lips found her ear.

"Please?" she whispered, and Jordan gasped when Alyssa's hand slid inside her underwear. She let her head fall back against Alyssa's shoulder, exposing her throat. "Do you *really* have to go?"

Jordan shook her head in response before she allowed Alyssa to push her onto her back. She was certain she was going to hate herself for it later, but she let Alyssa straddle her, because all she wanted to do was close her eyes and try like hell to convince herself it was Ash on top of her.

❖

Five hours later, Jordan found herself in line at the Starbucks located inside the Rio. Alyssa's idea of breakfast was a banana and a granola bar with orange juice to wash it down. Who the hell didn't have coffee with their breakfast? She didn't trust a woman who didn't drink coffee. Her plan for the day was to shower, sleep for about ten hours, and then hit the poker tables again. She was pulling money out of her pocket when a voice from behind startled her.

"Fancy meeting you here." Ash's smile faltered when Jordan turned to face her. "You look like hell, Jordan."

"Why, Miss Noble, you certainly know how to compliment a girl, don't you?"

"I'm sorry, but did you get any sleep at all last night?"

Jordan found herself at a crossroads. Did she want Ash to know she'd spent the night with a woman she'd just met? Especially after Ash found Tara in her room the night before, and it *wasn't* Tara she been with. She knew holding out any hope of a rekindling of their previous relationship was futile since Ash hadn't denied there was a girlfriend in her life. Not only that, but Jordan didn't want to get involved with anyone, did she? That imaginary line she drew for herself began to blur when Ash was in her hotel room. All she knew was she didn't want Ash to think she slept around.

"It's not a difficult question, Jordan. A simple yes or no would suffice. Did you get any sleep last night?"

"Smart ass." Jordan tried to hide a grin before turning serious. "No. A ghost from my past showed up at my door last night, and the emotions seeing her again brought to the surface made it a little difficult to sleep."

It wasn't really a lie. As exhausted as she was after a couple of hours with Alyssa, sleep eluded her. No matter how hard she tried, she couldn't get Ash's face out of her head. And having Ash there only led to memories of how good the sex had been between them. Poor Alyssa thought it was her causing Jordan to wake her again and again. When she'd tried to leave at four a.m., it was as much because she felt bad for using her as it was that she'd felt compelled to be alone to clear her head.

"I shouldn't have come to your room last night. I'm sorry." Ash looked like she wanted to bolt, but Jordan smiled to try to ease the tension between them.

"Not your fault, Ash. Honestly, I never expected to see you again. Having you show up out of nowhere kind of threw me for a loop." Jordan turned to place her order and didn't face Ash again until she'd gotten her bag containing a muffin, and her coffee. She was a little surprised to find her still standing there when she turned to leave the counter. "It is nice to see you again."

"Please," Ash said as she placed a hand on Jordan's arm. "Find a table and wait for me?"

Jordan nodded numbly and turned to locate a table inside the busy restaurant. She got lucky and saw a couple leaving. Her heart was racing so fast she wasn't sure she'd be able to eat the muffin she'd wanted so badly just ten minutes earlier. Once Ash finally joined her, Jordan found she couldn't look at her. Her biggest fear was that Ash would reject her—again. A thought she knew was crazy.

"Jordan?" Ash asked in a concerned voice.

The noise in the restaurant, so overwhelmingly loud only moments ago, seemed to become nothing more than background noise. Ash's attention was on Jordan's hand resting on the table. There was a slight tremor Ash noticed. She wondered if it was nerves, or if it had something to do with whatever was wrong with Jordan. Without thinking, she reached across the table and covered the hand with her own. She smiled when Jordan finally looked at her.

"What's wrong? Why did you leave the bureau?" Ash watched the emotions cross Jordan's face. She had the distinct feeling Jordan didn't even realize how easy she was to read. The hurt she understood. Ash knew it was her that had put that emotion there. The anger was understandable too. But the fear she saw before Jordan pulled away and began peeling the wrapper of her muffin was what scared her the most. "I know you told me you have muscle spasms, but that doesn't explain the tremor I just saw in your hand."

"Nerves," Jordan answered quickly. "You make me nervous."

"Bullshit," Ash said with conviction. "You were never nervous around me. Maybe if you had been..."

Ash let her voice trail off and felt like kicking herself. She just concentrated on unwrapping her own food and hoped Jordan would simply let it go. But of course she didn't. Jordan seemed incapable of letting anything go. Her FBI colleagues, while they'd been working a serial killer case together, jokingly referred to her as a dog with a bone.

"What?"

"What?" Ash shrugged as if she didn't know what Jordan was talking about. Jordan dropped her muffin and wiped her hands on a napkin.

"You said maybe if I had been nervous around you..." She paused and waited, causing Ash to squirm slightly. "What?"

What could she possibly say in response? *If you'd been nervous around me maybe I would have known it meant something to you? That I wasn't just a notch on your proverbial bedpost?* In reality, Ash didn't know either of those things to be true. At least not now, what seemed to be a lifetime later. At the time, Jordan bared her soul to Ash, something Ash knew was difficult for her. But it scared her senseless. How could she possibly leave the life she'd known forever to be with a woman?

If I'd only known then what I know now...

"Nothing. Just let it go."

The look on Jordan's face let Ash know she would do as she asked, but only for now. Jordan wasn't one to completely let things go. Especially when it came to Ashley. Not then, and apparently not now.

"You must work a brutal schedule if you were here last night and have to be back again this early," Jordan said before picking up her muffin again. "Your girlfriend must be very understanding if you spend your off time here too."

"I'm off today." Ash rested her forearms against the table and hung her head. This was stupid. Asking Jordan to join her at a show in the casino had seemed like a good idea before she'd left the house that morning, but now it seemed foolish. She couldn't figure out in her mind how to ask without it sounding like she wanted a date. And she needed to tell her she was single. Because no matter how hard she tried to convince herself otherwise, she *did* want this to be a date.

"Do you live in the hotel? Because that's the only reason I can think of for you to be here on your day off."

"No, I have a house in Henderson. Listen, Jordan, I let you believe I have a girlfriend. I should have told you the truth right away, but it seemed easier to just let it go. I'm single." She waited for a response, but Jordan was silent. She met Jordan's eyes and knew she just had to do it. Like pulling off a bandage. "I have tickets to a show tonight. You're welcome to come with me if you'd like."

Jordan smiled. It was the same damn smile Ash had told her did strange things to her belly. Ash looked away and closed her eyes against the onslaught of memories. How could that smile still affect her the same way?

"I would love to."

"You didn't even ask what show it is."

"It doesn't matter." Jordan's voice dropped an octave, and Ash was sure everyone in the restaurant could pick up on the nuance of what she was saying. "It never did with you, don't you know that?"

"Don't, Jordan."

"Don't what?"

"Don't read something more into it than there is."

"Am I?" Jordan wasn't sure if she was or not. The prospect of a date with Ash was as scary as it was exciting. "Because it sounds like you're asking me on a date."

"Not a date. We're just two old friends going to a show together."

"Okay, you can tell yourself that." Jordan nodded before popping a piece of her muffin into her mouth. She wondered briefly why it was so damn easy to flirt with Ash after so much time had passed. It really did seem to be the natural way for them to interact. Whether anything ever came of it or not. "What time should I meet you?"

"I'm not sure when I'll get here, so how about I just come to your room?"

"Sure." It certainly sounded like a date to Jordan.

CHAPTER EIGHT

Y ou asked her out on a date?"

"No, Oz, I'm pretty sure I specifically told her, and you, it is *not* a date," Ash said, holding the phone to her ear with her shoulder as she searched through her closet for something to wear. Despite her insistence on their evening only being about two friends catching a show together, it did feel like a date. But Ash didn't date. Dating meant you wanted to see the person again, and she hadn't done that since…"Jordan," she muttered under her breath.

"What? I didn't catch the last thing you said," Oz told her.

"I was just talking to Trixie."

"She doesn't talk back to you, does she?"

"Very funny."

"What happened to avoiding Jordan at all costs?"

"Well, it might have been possible had I not had to go in the cage last night while she was at the window." Ash tossed aside the only dress she owned. She had nothing against dresses, as long as they were on someone else. She only had this one because she lost a bet with Oz three years earlier. It was a pool game, and the loser had to wear a dress to work the next day. She had wanted so badly to beat him. That being said, it was the only time she'd ever lost to him at pool.

"So you just decided to hell with it and asked her out." Oz chuckled, and Ash could picture him shaking his head and trying not to laugh out loud. It did sound ridiculous when he said it.

"God, I'm so stupid," Ash said as she sat on the edge of the bed and Trixie sat on her lap. "I don't know what I was thinking."

Maybe she could call and cancel. Or just not show up. No, she needed to put on her big girl panties and follow through on the evening. When the show was over, Jordan would go back to her room and Ash would go home. Simple.

"I do. I saw her this afternoon when they called her name for an open seat at one of the poker tables. Have I ever told you you have exquisite taste in women?"

"More than once, yes. I figured you were just jealous."

"Oh, I am, trust me. Maybe I should let you find dates for me from now on."

"The women I'd find wouldn't be interested in you, Oz. I rarely even look at straight women anymore."

"That's a shame, because I've seen more than a few looking at you."

"I'm hanging up now," she said. She pushed the cat off her lap and ignored the indignant look Trixie gave her.

"Wait," Oz said. "I'm curious about something. Why does she use a cane?"

"I don't know. I asked her, but she just brushed it off."

"Then it's probably something serious. I had an uncle who said it was nothing, and three months later he was dead. Cancer. Make her tell you what's really going on, Ash."

They hung up after a couple more minutes of small talk, but Ash couldn't get what he'd said out of her mind. Cancer? Was it possible? No, she looked too healthy. But did that really mean anything at all? Most people looked healthy until they started chemo, right?

"Fuck, Noble, you're going to drive yourself crazy." She did her best to shut everything out and concentrate on getting herself ready for her date that was definitely *not* a date.

❖

Jordan was dismayed when her pulse quickened at the knock on her door. She stopped in front of the full-length mirror on the bathroom door and smoothed her hands down the front of the green blouse that made her eyes stand out. She smiled at her reflection and took a deep breath before turning and pulling the door open. What she saw made her heart skip a beat.

Ashley's dark blond hair was down around her shoulders, and her eyes seemed even more blue than Jordan recalled them being. The simple black and white pantsuit was obviously tailored to fit Ash and highlighted every curve Jordan's hands remembered so well. Her fingers twitched as she fought to not place her hands on Ash's hips and pull her close.

"Are you okay?" Ash asked. "You look a little strange."

"Fine," Jordan answered with a terse nod. She stepped aside and motioned for Ash to enter. Ash looked at her watch and then back down the hall toward the elevator before finally meeting Jordan's eyes.

"We should probably go."

"What time does the show start?"

"Seven thirty."

"Ash, it's not even six yet. Come in. I promise I won't bite."

Ash looked uncomfortable but entered the room. Jordan shut the door and followed her into the main seating area.

"I thought we might want to grab something to eat beforehand." Ash sat on the couch and proceeded to look everywhere in the room except at Jordan. "You can't always get a table right away in these restaurants."

"Then we'll order room service." Jordan stared at her for a moment but walked across the room to get the menu when Ash still refused to meet her eyes. "What do you feel like having?"

"It's too expensive, Jordan."

"I didn't ask you to pay." Jordan took a seat on the couch next to her and opened the menu. "I figured I was paying my own way, which reminds me. How much do I owe you for the ticket to the show?"

"Nothing," Ash said, her tone indicating Jordan had hurt her feelings by asking. "I get tickets to one of the shows each month. They were free."

"Cool."

"Did you really think I would make you pay for it?"

"I honestly didn't know. It's been a long time since I've spent an evening out with someone who was just a friend. This is foreign territory to me." Jordan looked at her, but Ash was picking at a loose thread on the arm of the couch. "Why are you so damned nervous?"

"I'm worried you think this is a date."

"You're worried I think it is, or you're worried *you* think it is?" Jordan watched her intently as Ash closed her eyes and swallowed audibly. Interesting, Jordan thought to herself. Maybe Ash wants it to be a date after all. *But it can't be. Not with my medical condition.* Jordan decided a change in topic was in order when it became apparent Ash wasn't going to respond. "How about the prime rib? Is it any good?"

"It's excellent," Ash said, finally turning to look at her.

When their eyes met, Jordan had the sensation of the room spinning, and she found it difficult to breathe. It felt as though the past fifteen years never happened. She knew it would be so easy to wrap her arms around Ash and pull her close.

"Prime rib for two, then," Jordan managed to say without her voice trembling like her hands were. When she turned away to grab the phone, she was finally able to breathe again. She ordered their dinners and a bottle of Shiraz to go along with it. When she was done she tossed the menu onto the coffee table and fell back into the cushions, her eyes closed.

"Are you all right?"

"I am," Jordan answered as she placed her hands under her thighs. "I hope it was okay with you that I ordered wine."

"It's perfect. I'm surprised you remembered Shiraz is my favorite."

"I told you last night, I remember more than I should about you."

Ash held her breath for a moment, bracing herself for when she'd come undone when their eyes met again. But Jordan didn't move. Just watching her like this caused a swarm of butterflies in Ash's stomach. No one else—*no one*—had ever caused that sensation. Not before Jordan, and certainly not after. She was surprised to find Jordan still had the same effect on her after all this time.

"I'm sorry, I think I just made things awkward, didn't I?" Jordan asked as she sat up straighter. Her hands were still under her thighs. Did she really think Ash hadn't noticed the way they were shaking? "And you came here last night to apologize for something, but I didn't let you do it. Feel free to do so now."

"You said last night I didn't need to apologize."

"I did." Jordan nodded and smiled at her. "But it occurred to me you might have had a speech all planned out. If you did, I want to hear it."

"No speech," Ash said. "Just a way to hopefully explain why I did what I did."

"Go ahead. The food won't be here for another twenty minutes, at least."

Ash sighed and leaned forward, her forearms resting on her thighs. She'd known the night before it wasn't going to be easy, but Jordan had let her off the hook. Now she didn't even know where to begin.

"You scared the hell out of me when you told me you loved me," Ash finally said, avoiding looking anywhere near Jordan.

"So you dumping me was my own fault?"

"No, I'm not saying that. Kevin would have killed you if he'd found out we were sleeping together."

"Then you dumped me to protect me."

"Jesus, Jordan. This sounded so much better in my head, mainly because you weren't interjecting your own commentary every other sentence." Ash stood and went to the windows overlooking the strip. She crossed her arms over her chest and closed her eyes. "You weren't supposed to fall in love with me. You knew my situation before we even kissed for the first time."

"You're right. I did," Jordan said. Ash didn't turn around when she heard Jordan stand and go to the minibar. A few seconds later, Jordan was at her side, handing her a glass of what looked like bourbon. "And as much as I tried not to fall in love with you, I'm sorry to say I didn't have any control over the situation."

Ash took the glass and downed most of it in one swallow. She let the burn of the alcohol suffuse her body before finishing what was left. She finally looked at Jordan and thought she saw longing in her eyes. Or maybe she was just seeing what she was hoping to see.

"Apparently, I didn't either."

Jordan looked out the window and sighed. Ash wanted to throw her arms around her and kiss her senseless, but she didn't. Even if Jordan responded, Ash sensed there was a barrier between them that wouldn't easily be brought down. Her heart ached for what might have been if she'd followed her heart fifteen years earlier.

Chapter Nine

Jordan woke the next morning with Ashley on her mind. Their evening had gone well once the dinner arrived. They didn't talk any more of the past they shared, but instead caught each other up on bits of their lives. After the show, Ash walked her back to her room and they shared a lingering embrace and a chaste kiss on the cheek. The few seconds their bodies were pressed together had fueled Jordan's dreams quite nicely. So much so that there was a persistent ache between her legs now.

Without thinking about what she was doing, she slid her right hand slowly down her abdomen and brushed the fingers of her left hand over a taut nipple. It sent a jolt through her body, and she let out a gasp when her fingers came in contact with her clit. She was wetter than she ever remembered being before. At least since the last time she'd been with Ash. Jordan stilled her fingers and held her breath as she stared up at the ceiling.

"What the fuck am I doing?" she asked no one. Ash had always been able to get under her skin, and apparently, fifteen years hadn't changed that fact. Jordan hadn't touched herself like this in a very long time. But spending the evening with Ash as a friend had been more frustrating than she'd thought it would be. She wiped her fingers on the sheets before forcing herself to get out of the bed. Being this turned on was unnerving, but knowing she *could* be just by thinking about a woman was invigorating. Thank God the MS hadn't taken away her sex drive like the doctor warned it might.

She smiled as she walked toward the bathroom but stopped when her cell phone rang. She picked it up off the nightstand and felt a surge of excitement when she saw Ash's name on the screen. They'd exchanged numbers the night before while they were eating dinner, and Jordan had programmed it into her phone as soon as Ash left.

"Good morning."

"Good morning to you," Ash said.

Jordan knew she had to be imagining it, but she could have sworn she heard a smile in Ash's voice. How odd. How could you possibly hear a smile?

"I didn't wake you, did I?"

"No, I've been up for a whole ten minutes already." Jordan opened a drawer and began pulling out the clothes she wanted to wear while she held the phone between her ear and her shoulder. "Why are you awake so early? I thought you had the day off."

"I do. I'm going to Hoover Dam with a friend today. I was wondering if you'd be interested in joining us."

Jordan stopped what she was doing and straightened. She didn't know what to say. Of course she wanted to spend more time with Ash, but who was the friend she mentioned? She had no interest in being a third wheel.

"She's my neighbor, and she's in a wheelchair. I bring her to Vegas a couple times a month for dinner. You're welcome to join us for dinner this evening too."

"Sure, why not?" Jordan said as she looked at her reflection in the mirror above the dresser. "I'd only hang out in the casino all day otherwise. My bank account would probably prefer a day of sightseeing."

Ash gave Jordan her home address and they hung up. Jordan looked again in the mirror. She'd kept herself in decent shape over the years. She was determined not to use her cane today, but she knew it would be foolish to leave the hotel without it. She couldn't get the image out of her mind of a woman in a wheelchair. She'd probably end up in one someday herself, but the thought of it scared the living hell out of her.

❖

"I finally get to meet the famous Jordan Stryker?"

"Jesus, Maria, she is not famous," Ash said as she led her into the living room so they could wait for Jordan to get there.

Maria Forman and her husband, Lance, lived next door to Ash. Lance routinely went on business trips to Phoenix and Los Angeles, and Ash agreed to keep an eye on Maria for him. She'd been diagnosed with multiple sclerosis almost fifteen years earlier, and had only been forced to spend the majority of her time in the motorized chair for the past six months. Maria needed someone to keep an eye on her because she tended to think she didn't need the chair and tried to do too much on her own. Maria also despised giving herself the injections of interferon she needed to keep the progress of her disease at a snail's pace. Ash couldn't really blame her on that front. The thought of sticking herself with a needle three days a week made her cringe inwardly.

"You seem nervous, Ash," Maria said.

"I'm not," she lied. The look Maria gave her indicated she didn't believe her for a second. Ash sighed and closed her eyes for a moment, resigning herself to the fact she wasn't going to be able to fool Maria. "I'm not sure how to act around her."

"What do you mean, honey?"

"I get flustered when she's anywhere near me. She makes my heart beat a little faster, and my hands shake."

"Sounds to me like you still love her." Maria folded her hands in her lap and sat back with what Ash could only describe as a self-satisfied smirk. "But I seem to recall you insisting you weren't in love with her before."

"That's what I told myself, and I even believed it until I finally realized I was comparing everyone to her."

"Sexually?"

"Sexually," Ash said with a nod before taking a deep breath. "And not. Nobody's ever been able to make me laugh like she does. And nobody's ever been able to turn me on with just a look."

Ash had the decency to blush at the statement, but it was true, and she'd known Maria long enough that she didn't have a problem telling her the truth about her feelings. Maria brought her chair closer and took Ash's hand in hers.

"Maybe you should tell her how you feel. You never know, she might feel the same way. You know I'm a firm believer in everything happens for a reason. Perhaps you two were meant to be together. Why else would she show up in Vegas out of the blue? And at your hotel?"

"Um, maybe because she's playing in the WSOP and it's being held at the hotel I work at?"

"Stop." Maria pulled her hands away and laughed as she slapped Ash's leg playfully. "You know what I mean. Why did she leave her job, and why poker?"

Why did she leave her job indeed. That was the million-dollar question, wasn't it? Ash made a vow to herself to find out the reasons.

❖

"It doesn't matter how many times I see it, it never fails to amaze me."

Ash looked in the rearview mirror and smiled at Maria, who always seemed to make the most out of every day. They'd been to the Hoover Dam so many times Ash had lost count, but Maria always said the same thing after they got back on the road and headed back to Henderson.

"It is amazing," Jordan said in agreement. "But the Dam has nothing on the Grand Canyon. I could look out over the rim every day and never get tired of it."

"Oh, Ashley, you have to take me there someday," Maria said.

"You've never been?" Jordan twisted in her seat to look back at her and Maria shook her head. Jordan looked at Ash. "You should have said something. We could have gone there instead. It's only about a four-hour trip."

"Maybe next Friday, if you aren't busy." Ash never took her eyes off the road. She was glad Jordan had warmed up to Maria as the day progressed. When she'd first arrived it seemed like she didn't want anything to do with her. Ash couldn't figure it out though, because the Jordan she remembered had always been at ease with everyone she met.

"My tournament ends Tuesday, and the next one doesn't start until Sunday. We can leave early and I'll do half the driving if you want."

Ash smiled and nodded. She fought the urge to reach out and place a hand on Jordan's thigh. It seemed like the natural thing to do, and that scared her. She gripped the steering wheel tightly and concentrated on driving.

"Ash, I think I just want to go home, if that's all right," Maria said when they got close to Henderson. Ash looked in the mirror in time to see Maria wink at her. "I'm pretty worn out, but you guys should go to dinner without me. Have fun."

Ash knew what Maria was doing. And if the grin on Jordan's face was any indication, she did too.

Chapter Ten

Y ou don't have to go to dinner with me if you don't want to," Jordan said after they'd dropped Maria off at her house. Jordan had experienced tingling and numbness in her legs and feet off and on for most of the day. She'd passed it off as her foot falling asleep more than once and said something about a pinched nerve in her lower back, which was a lie. Ash seemed to have taken her excuse at face value, but she'd felt Maria watching her curiously. She was relieved when Maria decided not to join them for dinner, but she also didn't want Ash to feel as though she had to spend more time with her.

"Two nights in a row would be too much for you?" Ash asked.

Jordan knew she was kidding her. The smirk gave her away. Jordan wished she didn't know her so well, but on the other hand, she wanted to get to know her so much better. But that was a bad idea. If she hadn't known it before, meeting Maria made it painfully obvious. She'd wind up in a wheelchair someday, and Ash deserved more than to be forced into caring for her that way.

"I don't think I'd ever get tired of spending time with you." Jordan couldn't have stopped the words even if she'd wanted to. Flirting seemed to come so naturally with Ash. And she'd say whatever she needed to say in order to get Ash to smile like she was now. "As friends, of course."

"Of course." She pulled into the driveway and shut off the ignition. "Let me just run inside and feed Trixie. You can go on ahead if you want. I can meet you at the hotel."

Jordan nodded before they both got out of the car. She watched Ash walk up to the front door and allowed herself to think for just a moment what it would be like to have a life with her. She shook her head. Fantasy was nice, but it had no place in the real world. A life with Ash wasn't meant to be. If it were, they'd have already celebrated their fifteenth anniversary.

❖

Jordan took a seat in the hotel lobby and waited for Ash to arrive. She knew she'd only be a few minutes behind her so there was no reason to make her way up to her room. Ash might think she was trying to get her alone. Jordan smiled at the thought.

"Is this a private moment, or would you care to share the reason you have such a huge grin on your face?"

Jordan looked to her left and saw Mark, the hotel employee who'd shown her to her room the day she arrived. He was dressed in street clothes this evening, and Jordan had to wonder. Was the Rio such a great place to work that all the employees spent their off time there? It made sense that the hotel would want them to spend their money here, but she couldn't imagine wanting to spend all her time in one place.

"It's a private moment," she answered and motioned for him to have a seat next to her. "I'm waiting for a friend. We're having dinner together."

"A friend?" Mark smiled. "You work fast, don't you?"

"It really is a friend. We hadn't seen each other in years when I ran into her the other night." Jordan wondered if Mark knew Ash. It would make sense if they did since they worked in the same hotel, but then again, there were probably so many employees there that everyone couldn't possibly know everyone else.

"Mark?"

They both looked up to see Ash standing in front of them. Ash smiled when Mark stood and gave her a hug. Jordan struggled to stand without giving away the fact her legs were cramping up. She smiled at the two of them. Maybe she should have gone up to her room to get her cane.

"You're coming on the Fourth, right?" Mark asked. "My grandmother will be so upset if you don't show up."

"I wouldn't miss one of your grandmother's barbecues for the world, Mark, you know that." Ash looked at Jordan and her expression warmed considerably. Jordan wondered if her cheeks were as flushed as they felt. "How do you know Jordan?"

"Mark showed me to my room the day I arrived." Jordan hoped to forestall any mention by Mark that he'd given her the address of a bar the night Ash had come to her room. He apparently got the message because he smiled and nodded once when she caught his eye.

"Well, I should get going. I'm meeting a friend for dinner too." He winked at Jordan before turning and disappearing into one of the many bars in the casino.

"So, where are we dining this evening?" Jordan asked.

"I thought we'd go out to the strip. Maybe the Rainforest Café?"

"I've never eaten there before." Jordan followed when Ash headed for the front door of the hotel. "I hear it's an interesting place."

"You're in for a treat if you've never been to one." Ash smiled at her and Jordan's pulse spiked. She had a feeling spending time with Ash was a big mistake. She wasn't sure how long she could keep her libido in check, and it was obvious by the way Ash looked at her she was interested in more than being just friends as well.

❖

Ash couldn't stop the smile at Jordan's expression when the lights in the restaurant dimmed and the animatronic rainforest animals came to life. She looked like a kid seeing Santa Claus for the first time.

"Wow," she said in obvious wonder when the show was over. "That was amazing."

"I love coming here with people who've never seen it before." Ash looked around the restaurant and laughed at the exuberance of one little girl enamored by the monkeys hanging from the tree above her table. "It never gets old."

"I hope you won't take this the wrong way, but you seem so much more relaxed than you did in LA," Jordan said.

"I am more relaxed than I was in LA." She knew Jordan expected her to become defensive, because that's what Ashley *Green* would have done. But Ashley *Noble* was more laid back. More of a take it as it comes kind of woman instead of someone who was constantly worried about what other people thought. Other people, meaning her parents and her husband. "I'm not sure if it was because I didn't belong in the police department, or if I was just so unhappy in my marriage, but I was wound way too tight back then."

"Don't I know it," Jordan said with a laugh.

Ash bit her bottom lip gently as she realized she'd come to a crossroads. Did she let the moment go, or did she take a chance and tell Jordan how she was feeling? Before she could contemplate it too much, she reached out and covered Jordan's hand with her own.

"I really am sorry, Jordan. You meant so much more to me than I ever let you know. Spending time with you now has made me realize how good things could have been between us if I'd only followed my heart instead of letting everyone else's expectations dictate the decisions I made." Ash was aware of how loud her pulse was pounding in her ears, and she was sure everyone in the restaurant had to be able to hear it too. She didn't remove her hand and Jordan didn't pull away from her, so she took that as a good sign. "I've missed you."

"Excuse me, ladies," their waiter said. They both sat back to allow him room to put their food on the table. "Enjoy your meal, and don't hesitate to let me know if you need anything."

When he was gone, Jordan stared at her steak for a moment before reaching for the salt and pepper. She'd been so hungry when they first arrived, and knew what she wanted to order after a cursory glance at the menu. But now she wasn't sure she could eat anything. She put her hands in her lap, where Ash couldn't see they were shaking. She knew how hard it had been for Ash to say what she'd said, and she couldn't just ignore it. Couldn't let it go and pretend they were just *friends* who were sharing a meal.

"I've missed you, too," Jordan finally said when their eyes met across the table. But as soon as the words were out there, she wished she'd kept her thoughts to herself. If Ash was hoping to pick up where they'd left off fifteen years ago, she was going to be disappointed. One-night stands were the new normal for Jordan since her diagnosis. It wouldn't be fair to anyone, let alone Ash, to expect them to be caretaker for someone in a wheelchair. She knew that's where she'd be somewhere down the road, but if it would be tomorrow or twenty years from now, she didn't know. It was the uncertainty of the disease that was so fucking unfair.

She'd never met anyone with MS until Maria. She'd spent what seemed like a million hours researching it online. She'd read too many brochures and articles to remember. Yet the ambiguity of what her future held scared the hell out of her, so how could she ever expect anyone else to be equipped to deal with it? While the medication she was on would slow the progression, it didn't change the fact it *would* progress, because there was no cure.

"Jordan?"

She opened her eyes without even realizing she'd closed them. The look on Ash's face was one of concern, and Jordan knew she'd probably asked her a question. She forced a smile and shook her head.

"I'm sorry, I just got a little lost there. What did you say?"

"I asked if you'd mind teaching me how to play poker sometime."

"Sure." She seasoned her steak before unfolding her napkin and putting it on her lap. "How about tonight? We can find a table here in the MGM and you can observe."

"I'd rather do it somewhere private. We could go back to my house, or to your room. I'm more of a hands-on learner."

Jordan almost choked on her steak. She downed most of her beer and motioned the waiter for another round. Yes, she could attest to the fact Ash was a hands-on learner. And what incredibly amazing hands they were, too. She wasn't entirely sure what she agreed to, but she nodded and Ash looked pleased with herself. She couldn't shake the feeling that their evening was headed down a dangerous path.

CHAPTER ELEVEN

Jordan looked scared to death as they walked into Ash's house later that evening. Ash led her to the dining room and handed her a deck of cards. She could see in Jordan's eyes that she was interested in rekindling what they had before, but her body language was telling Ash something completely different.

"I don't have any poker chips, sorry." Ash placed a beer on the table to Jordan's right and then took a seat to her left.

"No problem. Have you got any matchsticks, or pretzels?" Jordan shuffled the deck without looking up. Her hands were shaking, and Ash wanted nothing more than to ease her nervousness.

"No, I don't."

"Candy? Peanuts? Anything you would have a lot of."

"I have a jar of pennies."

"Excellent. I'll shuffle while you get it."

Ash went upstairs, wondering how she should play this. She wanted desperately to kiss Jordan, and the conflict was wreaking havoc with her. She never hesitated when she wanted someone, but Jordan was different. Jordan wasn't someone she wanted to have for a night or two. The thought made her stop abruptly right outside her bedroom door. A night or two was all she *ever* wanted from a woman.

"But then again, it's always been about Jordan," she murmured. Trixie meowed at her from the doorway and head-butted her in the shin. She reached down and absently scratched under her chin. Jordan was the one she'd always wanted. It didn't seem to make a difference to her body that she was the one who ended things between them, because her body had never forgotten the way Jordan touched her. The way she felt on top of her. The way Jordan could turn her on with nothing more than a few words.

She sat on the foot of the bed and tried to sort through her thoughts. Was it possible she was still in love with Jordan after all the years that had gone by? Before she left LA she would have said yes, but since moving to Vegas Ash had made it her mission to forget about Jordan and the train wreck her life had become after Jordan had left. She'd been doing just fine right up until their eyes met on the casino floor two nights ago. Now it was all she could do to not think about her nearly every waking moment.

She took a deep breath before grabbing the jar of pennies and heading back downstairs. She had to figure out a way to let Jordan know how she felt about her. Maybe it wouldn't be tonight, but it would have to be before she left Vegas, and Ash, behind again.

❖

"That was fun," Ash said two hours later after they'd moved from the dining room table to the couch in the living room. "I'm sorry I took so long to absorb everything you taught me."

"A couple hours isn't bad, trust me," Jordan said quietly. She was uncharacteristically nervous, and she didn't like the way it felt. Then again, Ashley had always made her nervous from the first time they'd met. All night, or at least since Ash had returned to the dining room with her jar of pennies, she'd had the feeling Ash wanted to kiss her. She supposed it was probably just a case of her projecting *her* desires, but more than once she'd caught Ash staring at her with a strange little grin. "I used to play with a group of guys from the FBI, and they spent weeks taking my money before I finally caught on to how to really play the game."

Ash laughed, and Jordan felt her stomach do a flip-flop. The flame of desire she'd first felt when they sat down to dinner was threatening to overwhelm her senses. She resolved to steel herself to rebuff a good night kiss should Ash attempt one, but it was easier said than done. Her body was reacting to Ash in ways she hadn't expected since she'd agreed to have dinner with her. She was so wet it was uncomfortable trying to sit without adjusting her hips every few minutes. She began to look forward to getting back to her hotel room and taking care of it. The sooner the better.

"Would you like another beer?" Ash asked as she grabbed their empty bottles from the coffee table.

"I should probably call a cab and get back to the hotel." Jordan wasn't convinced she wanted to leave, so how could she expect Ash to believe it when the tone of her voice was so unpersuasive.

"Don't be silly. I can drive you back to town. A cab will cost a fortune."

"We've been drinking."

"You don't trust me? I'm not drunk."

"I don't trust anyone when they've been drinking, so don't take it personally." Jordan could see by Ash's expression that she did take it personally. "I don't even trust myself to drive when I've been drinking."

"Then you'll stay here tonight." Ash's tone indicated she wouldn't let Jordan argue with her. Jordan couldn't help the smile she felt tugging at her lips. Ash tilted her head to one side. "What's so funny?"

"You haven't changed a bit," Jordan said. "You get an idea in your head and you're convinced things will go the way you want them to, and to hell with anyone else's opinion on the matter."

"That is how we ended up in bed together the first time, isn't it? I didn't hear you complaining about it then."

"I didn't. And I'm not complaining now. I just think it's funny how you haven't changed in all this time."

"But I have," Ash said, sitting on the other end of the couch and handing Jordan a beer before she twisted the cap off her own bottle. "I wasn't a lesbian then."

"Yes, you were," Jordan said with a nod. "You just weren't ready to admit it to yourself."

"I'm sorry."

"For what?"

"For hurting you. For not being strong enough to walk away from the safe little life I'd built for myself. You told me you loved me, and I'm sorry the most for not being able to tell you I loved you too."

They sat in silence then, and Jordan didn't know what to say. Ash had loved her? It was like a blow to the gut. How different would her life have been if Ash had only said those words to her back then? She stared at the bottle in her hands as she marveled at the fact she wasn't angry. Hurt, yes, but not angry.

"Say something, Jordan. You at a loss for words scares the hell out of me."

"I honestly don't know what to say."

"Yell at me, tell me how I screwed everything up. Say anything."

"You didn't screw anything up, Ashley. You did what you had to do for you at the time. It was the only thing you could have done. Coming out—admitting you're a lesbian—isn't something I, or anyone else for that matter, could force you to do. It's a solitary thing, and something you had to realize in your own time. You obviously did that, so I'd say everything happened just like it was supposed to."

"Damn you for being so understanding."

Jordan laughed at the incredulous look on Ash's face. She couldn't help it. She also couldn't help the growing need to pull Ash close and tell her everything would be all right. But it wouldn't. It *couldn't*. Not with a disease like multiple sclerosis lurking in the shadows. She would never ask, or expect, Ash to take on the role of caregiver. She'd never wanted to put anyone in that position, and she wouldn't do it now.

"I still do."

"What?" Jordan was pulled out of her thoughts by Ash's words, but she didn't know what Ash was talking about.

"I still love you." Ash's voice never wavered, and her eyes held Jordan's as she spoke. "I don't think I ever stopped loving you. I may have gone for a few days at a time without thinking about you, but you were always in my heart. Is there any chance for us?"

Jordan stared at her, so many thoughts running through her mind. The foremost thought was a resounding *no!* But she couldn't make herself say the word. Instead she took a deep breath and looked at her hands as she spoke.

"Things are complicated, Ash."

"Complicated? Things were *complicated* when I was married and we had an affair. How can things be complicated now? We're both single, right? Or do you have a wife waiting for you back home?"

"What? No, God, it's nothing like that." Jordan raked a hand through her hair and stared at the ceiling. "There's no one."

"Are you dying?"

"We're all dying, from the moment we're born," Jordan said without thinking how callous the words might sound. And how she was trying to avoid answering the direct question. MS wasn't a death sentence; she knew that. But it did steal your life, and your spirit, a little at a time, and there was no cure. She met Ash's concerned gaze and forced a smile. "No, I'm not dying."

"Then what could be so complicated?"

Jordan's determination to not tell anyone about her health problems was slowly dwindling. She needed to put some space between them so she could work on reinforcing the walls Ash was trying so hard to knock down.

"It's your health, isn't it? The reason you left the bureau?"

"I left the bureau because I needed to. I was getting burned out. I dealt with death on what seemed like a daily basis, and it was taking its toll on me. I had some money invested, and I just decided it was time to try something new."

"So you chose poker?" Ash smiled as she said the words, and Jordan was relieved to sense she was going to let the matter drop, at least for now. One thing she knew about Ash though—she'd bring it up again.

"I did. Why not? I get to travel, and I get to play a game I'm good at. No kidnapped, mutilated, or dead people to deal with. It's a no-brainer, isn't it?"

"If you say so." Ash shrugged. "I'll wait to see if you win before I can agree it's a game you're good at though."

Jordan chuckled as she reached into her pocket for her cell phone. She didn't think it would be a good idea to stay the night with Ash, especially now that she knew Ash had feelings for her. It would make it that much more difficult to keep a safe distance from her.

"What are you doing?"

"Calling a cab. I should go back to the hotel."

"Please stay. You can sleep on the couch if you're worried you can't control yourself."

Jordan whipped her head up and knew she probably looked like she'd been caught doing something she shouldn't be. Ash laughed at her as she stood.

"I'm worried about you controlling yourself, not me," Jordan said, impressing herself with her quick recovery.

"Right," Ash said, making it sound like the word had three syllables. She headed toward the stairs but glanced over her shoulder before she disappeared. "I'll get you a blanket and a pillow. Don't go anywhere."

"I don't think I could even if I wanted to," Jordan murmured under her breath. She shoved the phone back into her pocket and closed her eyes. She was in so much trouble.

CHAPTER TWELVE

How did you finally admit to yourself you were a lesbian?" Jordan asked when they sat back down at the dining room table to play a few more hands before turning in for the night. They hadn't put the pennies away earlier, and Ash noted her pile of pennies was substantially smaller than Jordan's.

Ash hadn't expected this particular question from her, but she admitted to herself she'd probably be curious too if she weren't the one being asked. She rested her elbows on the table and rotated the beer bottle she held in her hands.

"Truthfully, I'm pretty sure I knew I was a lesbian before I ever met you. I just didn't know it was a real option for me."

"You grew up in Los Angeles," Jordan said, a skeptical look on her face. "How could you not know it was an option?"

"I led a pretty sheltered life, Jordan. I was an only child, and my parents seemed to do everything they could to shield me from the evils of the world." Ash hated thinking about her parents. They'd been so close up until the day she'd come out to them. Or rather, the day Kevin outed her to them. "I went to bible camp every summer, and most of my free time during the school year was taken up by church activities. You know, the church never missed an opportunity to tell all the kids how homosexuality was a sin, and we'd burn in hell for eternity if we even associated with *those kinds of people.* I didn't realize it at the time, but I think all the kids who had to spend so much time with church activities leaned that way."

"So it was like one of those ex-gay camp type of things?"

"No, not really. Just a lot of preaching and trying to keep us on God's path. As long as none of us acted like we were attracted to someone of the same sex, there wasn't a problem."

"I'm afraid to ask, but what happened if you did?"

"I don't know. I always kept to myself and hardly even looked at anyone, let alone another girl. There was this one kid though, a boy, who wasn't ashamed of what he was. He always watched the other boys. They took him away for a few hours one day. We all wondered what they were doing to him, but when he came back he refused to talk about it."

"Sounds scary to me," Jordan said.

"It was. But life went on, and he was still gay. In junior high school I met Kevin and we started dating. My mother did everything she could to try to convince me he was the one for me. I'd never doubted her before, so why should I then?" Ash wished she could travel back in time and tell her younger self she didn't have to do everything her mother wanted her to. God, life would have been far less difficult if she'd been strong enough to stand up and refuse to be pushed into anything. "We dated all through high school, and when we graduated, we got married. It seemed the logical thing to do at the time."

"And then I had to show up and screw with everything you thought you knew about yourself." Jordan gave her a sad smile as she shook her head and looked intent on studying the label on the bottle she held.

"Meeting you definitely threw me for a loop, I'll admit it." Ash chuckled as she remembered the first time she'd laid eyes on Jordan Stryker. There was an instant attraction on both their parts. She could tell by the way Jordan watched everything she did. What she wouldn't give to have Jordan look at her like that now. "But you didn't do anything to change me or the way I thought. I wanted to be with you. Maybe even more than I'd ever wanted anything before."

"But you insisted to me you weren't a lesbian," Jordan pointed out.

"Yes, I did." Ash nodded. "I lied. To you and to myself. You did change the way I thought going forward. I still tried to make things work with Kevin, but it was never the same after you. I finally admitted to him I was a lesbian, and he was pissed. He didn't understand how I could have lied to him for so long."

"It didn't matter to him that you were lying to yourself too? That you were trying to be straight?"

"No. Nothing mattered to him except his own reputation. He had friends on the force. Good friends. Guys who he told I was gay, and they made it their mission to make my life a living hell." Ash shook her head at the memories of the verbal abuse she'd been subjected to during the final month of her employment in the LAPD. "He took it upon himself to tell my parents too. Suffice it to say that did not go well."

"I remember you telling me you were really close with your parents. You said you could talk to them about anything."

Jordan sat back in her chair and met Ash's gaze. Ash had to look away when the intensity became too much. She was breathing a little heavy, and she thought she noticed the pulse in Jordan's neck quicken. She wondered if Jordan had thought about what she'd said earlier and was maybe rethinking her stance on rekindling what they once had.

"I could, until then. Kevin painted me as the bad guy in it all. He claimed I'd been cheating on him, with women, from the very beginning. I mean since junior high beginning." Ash fought to keep her hatred toward her ex-husband in check. They probably could have split amicably had he not gone over the edge and ruined her career as well as running straight to her parents with the news their only child was a dyke.

"Were you?"

Ash knew she should probably be angry at Jordan for even asking, but she couldn't find the energy. Kevin had been the recipient of her animosity for so long now, there was little left over for anyone else. She smiled and covered Jordan's hand with her own.

"You really were the first woman I'd ever been with. And Kevin was the only man. There were two other women before I finally told him I was gay. I'm not proud of how many women I've been with since I moved to Vegas, but in LA, I was faithful until I met you."

Jordan couldn't look at her. She didn't pull her hand away, because it felt surprisingly nice to have this physical connection to Ash. She turned her hand palm up and laced their fingers together. Ash squeezed gently, and Jordan finally looked at her.

"I'm so sorry I fucked up your life," Jordan said.

"You didn't, Jordan. You helped me to see who I really was. But Kevin, that bastard took everything from me."

"How do you mean?"

"I resigned because the bullying got so bad. Every single day there would be snide remarks about the dyke. The carpet muncher. Every disgusting slur there is about lesbians, they used it against me. A couple of times it got physical too, but I handled it."

"Did you report the assholes?" What Jordan wouldn't have given to have been able to defend Ash when she needed it.

"I did." Ash nodded as she took a deep breath. "But the captain was one of Kevin's drinking buddies too. Everything got glossed over. I was told there were written reprimands in their files, but I highly doubt it. But honestly, that wasn't the worst of it.

"I haven't spoken to either of my parents in over six years. They had one five-minute conversation with me after Kevin outed me to them, and it was only to find out if what he told them was true." Ash took a long pull from her beer. "What I said didn't matter though, because they believed him. Of course they did. He was the son they never had. It wouldn't surprise me if he still goes to their house on holidays. Probably with a new wife or girlfriend.

"After I quit the police department, I moved here hoping to get a fresh start. I called my parents once to give them my address and phone number. To this day, I've never heard a word from them. That first year I sent birthday, anniversary, and holiday cards. Every single one of them were sent back marked *refused*. I finally got the hint and stopped sending them. I figure if they want to find me, they know where I am."

Jordan was taken aback by Ash's words. How was it possible that someone who had an almost perfect relationship with their parents could be completely shut out of their lives just because they were gay? Her own parents had been uncompromising in their belief that she was sick when she'd come out to them, but they never cut off all communication with her. As much as she'd hated her father, she knew he'd tried to do the best he could. Granted, his best wasn't as good as some people's worst, but at least he'd never severed all ties with her.

"I don't even know what to say." Jordan held her hand tighter and tried to smile even though she felt like she failed miserably. "You haven't tried again? Sometimes so much time goes by that neither party feels they can make the first move. Maybe it would be worth it to give them another call."

"No, I won't beg for them to talk to me. If they're okay with not having a daughter, then I'm okay with not having parents. Besides, I have new friends and family here now."

"That's pretty harsh, don't you think?"

"Not after the things they said to me, no." Ash pulled her hand away and sat back in her chair. She grabbed the deck of cards and started shuffling. Without looking at Jordan she said, "Let's play some more, because I really don't want to talk about this anymore tonight."

Jordan nodded and put her ante in the pot. She would never force Ash to talk about anything she didn't want to, so if she wanted to change the subject that was fine with Jordan. She just wished she could have ten minutes alone with the three people who had hurt Ash the most. She mentally stepped back for a moment, wondering where the need to protect Ash had come from. She hadn't felt that since…well, since Ash.

Keeping her at arm's length was going to be much harder than Jordan had originally thought.

Chapter Thirteen

Ash woke up the next morning feeling decidedly unrested. It was probably because she hadn't been able to sleep very well knowing Jordan was on her couch downstairs. She was now on her back, one arm above her head, staring at the ceiling. Her breathing was a little erratic thanks to the erotic dream she'd had right before waking this last time. She absently scratched Trixie's chin as she thought about how she'd made a fool of herself the night before.

"She's probably already left. Couldn't bear to face me after I told her I still loved her," she said to the empty room. Trixie stopped purring and meowed at her. Ash looked over at the cat by her side. "You'd probably leave me too if you could, wouldn't you?"

The response was more purring and a surprisingly strong head butt to the chin. Ash kissed the cat on the top of the head before getting up to shower and brush her teeth. At least she wouldn't let Jordan see her in her sleeping T-shirt and shorts. That would probably scare her away if she'd decided to hang out to see her this morning.

Fifteen minutes later, she was headed down the stairs, and the smell of bacon frying wafted up to greet her. She watched in wonder as Trixie trotted ahead of her and went right into the kitchen, her tail straight up in the air. Ash called out when she saw Jordan bending down to pet the cat.

"I wouldn't do that if I were you."

"And why would that be?" Jordan stopped mid-stoop and straightened before looking toward the stairway.

"She doesn't like people."

"Neither do I, so we should get along just fine." Jordan smiled and reached down to give Trixie a scratch under the chin before turning back to tend the bacon. "Besides, she slept with me for most of the night, curled right up on my chest with her head resting on my neck."

"Really," Ash said. She looked at Trixie in wonder. She *never* liked anyone the first time she met them. Hell, it had taken Trixie months to warm up to *her* when she'd first brought her home.

"I hope it was okay to make you breakfast. There wasn't really a lot to choose from so you're getting a cheese omelet, some bacon, and one piece of toast. You do know what grocery stores are for, right?"

"It's perfectly okay. Thank you." Ash decided to ignore the remark about the grocery store. Had she known Jordan would be cooking her breakfast, she would have made a point of stocking up on some things. She pulled a chair out from the table and sat so she could watch her cook. "You don't really hate people, do you?"

"Not *all* people." Jordan glanced at her and winked, which caused a stirring in Ash's center. "Just the vast majority. Some of them are okay."

"You seem to be in a pretty good mood this morning." No doubt it wasn't because of anything Ash had said the night before.

"I am in a good mood, Ms. Noble. My first tourney starts tomorrow, and I'm excited to take everyone's chips. If I win, I'm buying a seat at the Main Event."

"You're counting on the money to enter?"

"No," Jordan said as she finished buttering the toast and brought their plates to the table. "I just figured there'd be no reason to enter the Main Event if I get embarrassed in my first tournament. Do you think I could afford to stay indefinitely at the Rio if I didn't have money?"

"No, I just wasn't sure why'd you be waiting on the outcome of one tournament before registering for the Main Event." Ash sprinkled some salt and pepper on her omelet before grabbing a slice of bacon and devouring it. She stopped chewing when she heard Jordan laugh.

"What?" she asked, her cheeks burning.

"Hungry?"

"I love breakfast," she admitted sheepishly. "What can I say? I could eat breakfast three times a day every day. Especially when there's bacon involved."

"Superman has kryptonite, and Ashley Noble has bacon?" Jordan arched one eyebrow and Ash almost choked on her food. How could she be so damned sexy and be seemingly unaware of the effect she was having on Ash's hormones?

"Pretty much, yeah."

"Good to know."

Ash was quiet as she concentrated on eating her breakfast and not staring at Jordan. She waited until they were done and the dishes were in the sink before trying to gather her thoughts, but Jordan squeezed her hand gently before walking past her into the living room. When Ash was able to make her feet cooperate so she could follow her, she saw Jordan was tying her shoes.

"Thanks for letting me crash on your couch last night."

"No problem."

"I should probably go since I'm sure you're working today."

"I don't have to go in until three if you want to just hang out for a bit." Ash didn't want her to go, but she wasn't sure how to convey the fact without sounding needy.

"No, I really should try to get my head into the reason I came here in the first place. Don't worry about giving me a ride though. I called and ordered a cab earlier. It should be here in a few minutes."

"You didn't have to do that."

Ash watched as Jordan checked her pockets to make sure she had everything. When their eyes met, it was as though all the air had been sucked out of the room. Ash took a step toward her, but Jordan shook her head once and looked away.

"I should wait outside," Jordan said, her voice sounding strained even to her own ears. All she had to do was walk past Ash and out the front door. Why did it sound so easy when walking away from her was the most difficult thing she could imagine? What she really wanted was to take Ash in her arms and kiss her until they were both breathless. In fact, it's what she'd wanted to do from the moment she'd seen Ash on the casino floor three nights earlier. She forced herself to walk past Ash without looking at her.

"Jordan," Ash said as she put a hand around Jordan's wrist. Jordan closed her eyes briefly before turning to face her. "I'm sorry if I made you uncomfortable last night. I just wanted you to know how I felt."

"No worries. It's fine. I'm glad you told me." Jordan didn't try to pull away, and Ash tightened her hold. Jordan didn't even think about what she was doing as she pressed Ash against the wall and slid a thigh between her legs. Before she could stop herself, she covered Ash's mouth with her own and moaned when Ash began a slow thrust against her leg.

Ash threaded her fingers through Jordan's hair and held her there as though she thought Jordan might pull away. There was no need though, because all rational thought escaped her, and Jordan had no intention of stopping something that felt so *right*. She pressed her body against her as Ash rode her thigh in a rhythm meant to gradually bring her to orgasm.

Jordan gasped when she felt Ash's hand move to her ass before going under her shirt and then up her torso and brushing lightly over her nipple. Ash smiled against her mouth and pinched the nipple between her thumb and forefinger.

"Jesus, Ash. You feel so fucking good," Jordan whispered when she pulled away from the kiss, her breath ragged. She tried her best to ignore the nagging voice in the back of her mind telling her this was a bad idea. With her body pressed tight against Ash's, she had a hard time remembering *why* this could possibly be anything but a good idea.

"Don't stop," Ash pleaded.

Jordan didn't make her ask again. She felt a rush of liquid heat between her legs when Ash slid her tongue between her lips. She whimpered. Or had it been Ash? Did it really matter? All that seemed to matter was the feel of Ash in her arms, in her mouth, and rubbing frantically against her thigh. It would have been so easy to ignore the horn honking from the driveway. The taxi. The thought of it snapped Jordan back to reality and she pulled away, not able to hide the rapid rise and fall of her chest.

"Please, baby, send the cab away. I'll take you to town when I go to work."

Jordan shook her head but never broke their eye contact. "What do you want from me, Ash?"

"I just want you." She reached for Jordan's hand, but Jordan took a step backward. "Underneath me. Or on top of me. I don't really care as long as we're both naked."

"No," Jordan said. Saying it confused her, because she wanted to say yes. She really wanted to just throw caution to the wind and drag Ash up the stairs to her bedroom. But then what would happen when the fire was extinguished? Could it ever really be extinguished with Ash? Jordan had her doubts. She turned toward the door. "I need to go."

"Jordan." Ash was pleading again, and Jordan couldn't help herself. She looked at her. "I need you."

"What happens when I'm done playing poker and go back home?"

"I don't know. All I know is right now. We can just have fun while you're here, if that's all you want."

"Really? You'd be happy with that?" Jordan knew she could never be, and she wasn't convinced Ash could be either.

"If that's all you can give me, yes. We were good together once, Jordan. You know we could be again. Just think about it."

Jordan didn't need to think about it. Leaving Ash fifteen years ago had shattered her heart. If they started sleeping together now and she had to leave her again, it might just kill her.

CHAPTER FOURTEEN

P romise me you'll think about it." Ash couldn't believe she was begging. She never had to beg anyone for anything. But Jordan was different, and deep down, Ash had always known it. She pushed away from the wall and closed the distance between them. "I get off work tonight at midnight. Can we get together for a drink?"

"I'll call you," Jordan said, but Ash could see in her eyes she was only telling her that to placate her. The cabbie honked his horn again, a little longer than the first time. Apparently, he was impatient. Jordan looked toward the door and Ash brushed past her into the kitchen.

"See you later," she said. She could feel tears threatening to fall, but she had no intention of letting Jordan see her cry. She stood at the sink with her back to Jordan. It was almost a full minute before she heard the front door open. When it closed again, the tears finally began to fall. Three days ago, she'd been in complete control of her life. What the hell happened between then and now? When Jordan walked into her life the first time, it had changed Ashley forever. Now she was back, and Ash felt like her whole world was off its axis all over again.

She roughly wiped the tears off her face and picked up Trixie, who was meowing and rubbing against her legs. She held the cat as Trixie nuzzled her neck and Ash smiled at the loud purring. When everything was falling apart, she could always count on Trixie to be there with the unconditional love only animals were capable of.

"I've got to start thinking about getting ready for work, baby girl," she said quietly. Trixie didn't seem to care though. She continued nuzzling Ash until she finally set her back down. "Maybe if I don't think about her it will all miraculously go away."

❖

"What's wrong with you today?" Jan asked around six that evening when they ran into each other at the cashier cage. "You don't seem like yourself."

"Who else would I be?" Ash asked with a weak smile. She shrugged in an attempt to downplay her morose mood. She'd tried calling Jordan three times, but it always went straight to voicemail. She was having a difficult time not feeling desperate. "It's just hard coming back to work after a couple of days off sometimes, you know? Especially with this damn poker tournament going on. Things aren't going to get back to normal around here for almost three more weeks."

"No, I've seen your beginning of the work week moods. That's not what this is, Ash." Jan surveyed the casino floor while Ash assumed she was waiting for a response. "You know you can talk to me, right?"

"I do know that, but this isn't the time, Jan." Ash hated that she couldn't keep her gaze from wandering to the poker room. She'd been through there five times in the past two hours looking for Jordan, but she wasn't anywhere to be found. She forced herself to meet Jan's eyes. "And besides, there's nothing to talk about."

"Is it Jordan?"

"Excuse me?" She tried to keep her expression neutral, but she could tell by Jan's smile she'd failed.

"I thought you were going to do everything you could to steer clear of her."

Ash was saved from answering by a voice in her ear.

"Hey, boss, you there?" It was one of the employees tasked with keeping an eye on all the security monitors. Ash didn't envy them the job. She'd go crazy if she had to sit and watch those feeds day in and day out.

"Go ahead, Bobby," she said into the small microphone attached to her wrist.

"We've got what looks like a card counter on blackjack table nine. Older bald man wearing blue jeans and the ugliest Hawaiian shirt I've ever seen, bar none."

"Roger that," she said before motioning for Jan to follow her to the pit. She knew Jan heard their conversation through her own earpiece so there was no need to fill her in. It didn't take Ash long to find the guy Bobby described. The shirt was indeed ugly, and she doubted he'd gotten it in Hawaii. It was covered with orange pineapples and purple coconuts. She shook her head as she walked to the table and placed a hand on the dealer's shoulder. She smiled at the guests seated around the table. "Excuse us for just a moment, folks."

"He's won like eight hands in a row," the dealer said when they were a few feet away. "He stays with cards most people would either split or double-down on, and he takes more cards when any rational person would stay."

Ash glanced at the young man's nametag and nodded, being careful not to look at the guy they were talking about. She liked to know all the casino employees by name, but there were new people coming in all the time, and with the number of employees, she was pretty sure it was impossible for anyone to know all of them.

"All right, Ryan, I'm going to be standing back watching for a few minutes. Just keep doing what you're doing like nothing's out of the ordinary." She waited for him to nod his understanding and then sent him back to the table. Ash went and stood next to Jan.

"New dealer?" Jan asked.

"Yeah, but he did the right thing to signal the camera when he suspected a counter." Ash was relieved. A lot of the new dealers just let things like that go because they weren't confident in their abilities to pick out a card counter.

"So what's the plan?" Jan asked as she turned her head away from both Ash and table nine.

"Observe for now," Ash answered. The key was to not let the guy know they were watching him. She glanced to her right and thought she saw Jordan heading for the elevators going up to the hotel rooms. She fought the urge to go after her. Once she was done with this guy maybe she'd try to call her again.

Ten minutes went by and Ash heard Bobby in her ear telling her to make her move because it looked like he was getting ready to pack it in. The guy had won six more hands in a row to the tune of five grand. She motioned for Jan to go around one way and she went the other so they were both standing behind him.

"Excuse me, sir, could you please come with me?" Ash asked as she leaned in close to his ear. He jerked his head around to look at her and when he realized she was casino security, he tried to get away in the other direction only to be met with Jan's smiling face. "We can do this quietly, or I can call in a few more people and we'll all accompany you out the front doors. Completely up to you, sir."

"What's this all about?" he asked looking back and forth between them. "I haven't done anything wrong."

"On the contrary, counting cards may not be illegal, but it can get you thrown out and banned from playing blackjack in this casino ever again." Ash could tell he wasn't going to go quietly so she raised her wrist to her mouth. "I need Lars, Bobby, and Mike at table nine to assist in escorting someone outside."

"You got it, boss," Bobby's voice said in her ear.

Ash heard Jan chuckle, but ignored her. They both knew nobody was coming to help, but the guy counting cards didn't know it. But if she knew Lars, he'd be standing somewhere not too far away in case they really did need backup. Hawaiian shirt guy sighed loudly and his shoulders drooped before he reached out to pick up his chips.

It irked Ash that she couldn't take his money but she stood patiently as she watched him shove the chips in his pockets. When he was finished, he finally got to his feet and went with them as everyone in the vicinity was pointing and whispering.

"The front doors are that way," he said as they walked him toward the cashier booth. "I thought you were throwing me out."

"Oh, I assure you, you've already been thrown out not only from the Rio, but from most of the casinos in town because they'll all have your name and photo in a matter of minutes," Ash informed him with a smile. "I just thought you might like to cash in your chips so you have absolutely no reason to come back here."

❖

Jordan was too keyed up to just sit in her room watching television all night. She'd gone down to play poker in the afternoon but came back to her room a little after six. She couldn't stop thinking about Ash. About the kiss. And about how she'd almost let her guard down and allowed things to go further than they should. She hated that she was so weak when it came to Ashley.

When had her life become such a fucked up mess? She didn't have to think too hard to come up with an answer. It had been the day she'd walked into that LA precinct and first laid eyes on Ashley Noble. Well, Ashley *Green* back then. The fact Ash had a husband was a non-issue even though Jordan had sworn to stay away from straight women. Apparently, it had been a non-issue for Ash too, at least at the onset, because they'd only known each other a week before their affair started.

Four months later, they'd captured their serial killer and Jordan's team was no longer needed in Los Angeles. At some point during their time together, Ash must have started to feel guilty because she'd mention Kevin every once in a while. And she'd be sure to reiterate how happily married they were.

The day before Jordan was scheduled to fly back to Portland they'd been in her hotel room. Naked and wrapped in Ash's arms, thoroughly sated and relaxed, Jordan couldn't hold back her feelings any longer. She uttered the three little words she'd never said to another woman before or since.

Ash had stiffened and stopped breathing for a moment or two, but she hadn't freaked out like Jordan was worried she would. Ash simply told her in no uncertain terms the same thing she'd told her before the first time they'd slept together— that she wasn't going to leave her husband. Oh, and that she thought it would be best if they never spoke to or saw each other again. Ever. Then she'd jumped out of bed and quickly dressed before hurrying out the door.

Jordan had had such a feeling of intense pain in her chest after the door closed, she'd been certain her heart was broken in two. She'd briefly thought about running after her, but what would that have accomplished? She'd told Ash after their first incredibly sensuous kiss that she could set the pace, and the rules, for their affair. Wasn't this just another rule?

As much as Jordan hated it, she'd abided by Ash's wishes. But that didn't mean she forgot about her. In fact just the opposite. She tried once or twice to have relationships with women, but inevitably she'd compare them to Ash. And nobody could ever measure up. She'd had crushes on women in high school and after, but Ash had been her first real love. And if she were to be completely honest with herself, she'd never been totally convinced Ash hadn't had feelings for her too.

She felt no satisfaction now that she'd been right.

Jordan jumped when her phone vibrated in her pocket. She pulled it out and saw it was Ash, but she set it down and let it go to voicemail. She'd called three other times since Jordan left her house that morning, and Jordan had ignored it every time. She hadn't even listened to the messages she'd left. What would be the point? What happened that morning could never happen again. No matter how much Jordan wanted it to, she knew it would completely wreck her to have to leave Ash again.

She ran her hands through her hair before making her way into the bathroom. She pulled the auto-injector out of the small bag she used to carry her toiletries and slid in the syringe holding the medication she hoped would keep her out of a wheelchair for the next twenty years or so. She held her own gaze in the mirror as she put the injector against her thigh and pressed the button. She winced at the prick of the needle going into her skin, but at least this was just a sub-Q injection where the medicine went right under the skin. She didn't think she could handle an injection into the muscle when she had to do it three times a week.

And she was thankful she didn't suffer from the nausea and chills she'd experienced for the first few weeks of doing the injections. It had been so bad that more than once during those initial weeks she'd wished for death. It still happened once in a while, but with nowhere near the intensity it had in the beginning.

She dropped the used syringe into the small medical waste receptacle she'd brought in her suitcase before setting the auto-injector on the counter. She had to get out of there. Out of her room, out of the hotel, out of the building altogether. Knowing Ash was somewhere in the casino excited her while simultaneously making her nervous as hell.

A bite to eat and a couple of mindless hours playing video poker somewhere was suddenly sounding good to her. She intended to be back early though, because she had a tournament to play the next day.

Chapter Fifteen

"Come to the club with me, Ash. I'll even buy the drinks."

"Not tonight, but thanks for the offer," Ash said to Jan as she gathered her things and got ready to knock off for the day. "I'm beat. I just want to head home and sleep until I have to come in tomorrow."

"You know it's not going to do you any good to sit at home waiting for her to call, right?" Jan slung her purse over her shoulder and held the door for Ash.

"Excuse me?" Ash had to speak louder now that they were on the casino floor. She was beginning to hate the sounds of all the slot machines making noise at once. It was always worse on the weekends, and this being Saturday night, it was almost deafening.

"How many times did you call her? Two? Three? I mean if she wanted to talk to you don't you think she would have answered at some point?"

Ash shook her head and walked away before she had the chance to really go off on Jan. It was one thing to be a friend, but quite another to try to insert yourself into someone else's personal life. As far as Ash was concerned, it was none of Jan's business what she did with her time away from work.

"Hey, I'm sorry, all right?" Jan said when they walked into the employee parking garage. It was quieter there, so at least they didn't have to yell in order to be heard. "I'm just worried about you. In all the years I've known you, I've never seen you this out of sorts over a woman, or anything else, for that matter."

"I'm fine, okay? I'm going to go home, shower, and then fall into bed where I intend to be asleep before my head even hits the pillow, if that's at all possible outside of a novel." Ash had no intention of telling Jan the reason she was so beat was because she hadn't been able to sleep the night before knowing Jordan was downstairs on her couch. "I'm really okay."

"All right. Just call if you need to talk about anything." Jan pressed the button to unlock her car, but Ash never slowed down. "I guess I'll see you tomorrow then."

"Yep," Ash said as she pulled out her cell phone to see if Jordan had called and she'd somehow missed it. Nothing. She got in her car and debated with herself whether to call again. Five times in one day might be bordering on obsessive. Hell, four times might be, and she'd already hit that mark, so what was one more? And Jordan had said she'd call about getting together for a drink, right? She sat there for a good fifteen minutes debating with herself as to what she should do. She finally pressed the button then held the phone to her ear but didn't start the car yet.

She was about to hang up after it rang five times, assuming it would just go to voicemail again, but then it was answered, and Ash could hear pulsating dance music playing in the background. She held the phone away from her ear for a moment.

"Yeah?"

"Jordan?" Ash asked. It sounded like her, but she'd never answered the phone that way before. "Is that you?"

"Who else would it be?" she asked, obviously trying very hard not to slur her words. She spoke very slowly and deliberately. "Where are you?"

There was silence from Jordan, and Ash could hear the music playing. She hoped Jordan was going outside where she could hear better, but it soon became apparent that wasn't the case. The music wasn't getting any quieter.

"Jordan, are you there?"

"Yes, I am. Who is this?"

"It's Ashley."

"Right! Ashley Noble. What a noble name you have." Jordan began to laugh at her own joke, lame as it was.

"Jordan, where are you?" Ash couldn't keep her voice from rising, hoping to get through to her by sheer force if nothing else.

"Good question. Let me ask someone."

Ash sighed in exasperation as she listened to Jordan trying to get the bartender's attention. Everything was muffled then and she apparently held the phone to some part of her body as she was conversing with someone.

"Slick!" Jordan shouted into her ear a moment later. "I'm told the name of this bar is Slick. That sounds a little erotic, doesn't it?"

"I'll be there in fifteen minutes. Don't go anywhere."

Ash disconnected the call and tossed the phone onto the passenger seat before setting off to her destination. Slick was where Jan was going. Ash knew if Jan set her sights on Jordan, she'd probably end up going home with her. Jan wouldn't care if Jordan was drunk off her ass.

Fifteen minutes later, she walked into the bar and scanned the immediate area for Jordan. She finally saw her sitting at the bar about halfway down, and sure enough, Jan was right next to her, one hand low on Jordan's back, as she leaned closer to speak directly into her ear. Ash decided to hang back for a minute and see what developed. She ordered a beer and stood back from the bar to drink it.

Ash watched with interest as Jan kept leaning in close and laughing, but Jordan kept pulling away from her, shaking her head at whatever Jan was saying. At one point Jan seemed to be getting a little too friendly and Ash saw Jordan reach down below the bar and push what she assumed to be Jan's hand away from her body. After a few minutes, Jan stood and threw her hands in the air as if to say she was giving up. She grabbed her drink and stalked away, looking for her next victim.

Ash took a deep breath and silently cheered Jordan for apparently blowing Jan off. Even drunk she had good taste. She began to make her way over to Jordan and took the barstool Jan had vacated. Jordan was resting her head on her arms, but she obviously felt that someone had taken the seat next to her.

"Jesus H. Christ, why can't you just take no for an answer?" Jordan didn't lift her head to see who was there.

"I don't remember you telling me no," Ash said. Jordan didn't move, but she jumped slightly at the sound of her voice.

"Ash, is that you?"

"Yes, it's me. Did you drive here?"

"Taxi." Jordan finally sat up, but Ash thought it might have been better for her if she hadn't. She looked to be a little green around the gills.

"If she throws up on my bar you'll be paying for the cleanup, Ash," said Red, the head bartender. Ash looked at her and nodded. She'd earned the nickname because of the color she dyed her hair. Most days it was so red it was almost purple. "You know her? Because you usually don't go for the ones who are already plastered."

"I knew her when I was living in Los Angeles. She's a friend. Does she have a tab I need to settle before I get her out of here?"

"Nope, she gave me her credit card. I'll grab it for you."

"Jordan," Ash said, but she'd put her head down again. She put a hand on her shoulder and gently shook her. "Jordan, come on, we're leaving."

Nothing. Great, she was passed out. Red handed her the credit card, which she shoved into her pocket before grabbing Red's arm to keep her from walking away.

"Can you help me get her to the car? I think she's passed out."

Red stood there for a moment, her hands on her hips as she studied Ash's face. She shook her head and looked at Jordan.

"You can do better than this, Ash," she said. "Hell, you do better most nights you come in here. I've never seen you leave with someone this wasted."

"She really is a friend, Red, not a quick hookup," Ash said. She resented having to defend herself to someone she hardly knew. Someone she only knew from coming into the bar. "Can you help me or not?"

Red shrugged and hollered down to the other bartender on duty to cover for her. She came under the bar and lifted Jordan in her arms as if she weighed nothing. Ash motioned for her to follow her outside. Once there, Ash stopped, remembering her car was parked a couple blocks away.

"I'll get the car and be back in a couple of minutes." Ash apologized and Red was muttering what she was sure were obscenities under her breath. Luckily, there was a bench on the sidewalk and Red set Jordan down to wait. "I'll be right back."

Ash took off running down the street, musing how she'd never noticed Red was so muscular before tonight. She'd tried to pick Ash up on more than one occasion, but Ash told her about her rule concerning locals. Besides, she was much too young for Ash at only twenty-five. Red was only the head bartender because her sister owned the place, not because she'd earned it by spending years doing the job.

When Ash pulled up to the curb in front of Slick, she saw Jordan trying to push Red away, but Red was trying to pick her up again to get her into Ash's car. Ash jumped out and ran over to them.

"Jordan, she's trying to help you, all right?" Ash said, gripping her jaw so she'd hold her head still and look at her. When she finally did, Jordan's eyes softened and she nodded her head slightly. "Will you let her help?"

"Yeah," Jordan said, sounding dejected. Red picked her up again and Ash hurried to open the passenger side door for her.

After Jordan was securely buckled in, Ash shut the door and turned to face Red.

"If she drinks like that all the time, I don't want her in here again."

"She usually doesn't drink much at all," Ash assured her. She couldn't help but think this was her fault. Jordan had told her at dinner the night before she usually didn't drink much because she was worried her mother's dementia was caused by alcohol, and the last thing Jordan wanted was to end up like her mother. Had Ash pushed her over the edge by telling her she still loved her? Was it possible she was drinking herself into a stupor to try to forget Ash? She hoped not, but what else could have driven her to drink this much?

❖

Jordan fell asleep on the drive back to the hotel, but by the time Ash pulled into the parking garage at the Rio, she was at least conscious again. Getting her up to her room would have been a nightmare had she still been passed out. As it was, they didn't look too out of place walking to the elevator amongst all the other people who had been there all night drinking and gambling.

Ash didn't try to engage her in conversation because the couple of things Jordan had said in the car were unintelligible. All she wanted to do was get her safely to her room and put her to bed. Then she was dragging her ass home to sleep.

She sat Jordan on the end of the bed and began looking through her things to find something for her to sleep in. She wasn't having any luck though and finally closed the last drawer in frustration before raking a hand through her hair and turning toward Jordan.

"Pajamas?"

Jordan only shook her head and then closed her eyes as though doing so was a bad idea. Ash half expected her to fall onto her back, but instead she placed both hands firmly on the mattress and tried to stand.

"What are you doing?"

"Bathroom," Jordan answered slowly, but with the way she was slurring her words it came out more like *bafroo*.

"Your pajamas are in the bathroom?" Ash asked and was given a very careful nod in response. "Do you need to pee?"

"No. Sleep."

"All right, I'll go get them. You wait right here." She hurried into the other room and found a T-shirt hanging on the towel rack with a pair of shorts. Since they were the only clothes she could see, she grabbed them and turned toward the mirror above the sinks. She almost dropped the clothes when she saw the medication sitting on the counter.

Interferon. She didn't know brand names, but that word was prominent on the box, and she knew what it was for. Multiple sclerosis. She knew because it was what Maria injected three times a week. There was also one of those auto-injectors next to the box.

"Fuck," she said under her breath as things suddenly made sense to her. Why Jordan had been uncomfortable around Maria. Why she sometimes walked with a cane. Why her only explanation as to why they couldn't get together was *it's complicated.*

"Ash," Jordan called from the other room. Ash quickly tossed a towel over the medication. Obviously, Jordan didn't want anyone to know about it, and it would probably be even worse if she knew Ash had stumbled across it accidentally. Hopefully, she was drunk enough she wouldn't even think about it in the morning.

She plastered a smile on her face and exited the bathroom to find Jordan trying to make coffee. After tossing the clothes on the bed, Ash took her by the arm and had her sit on the couch. It was an awkward maneuver, and Jordan nearly succeeded in pulling Ash down on top of her.

"I want coffee." Jordan pouted, sticking her bottom lip out.

"I'll make it for you." Ash placed the prepackaged filter in the machine as she talked. She needed any diversion she could get to keep from thinking about Jordan being sick. "You just relax, all right?"

Jordan only grunted in response. Once Ash had the coffee brewing, she looked toward the couch and saw Jordan was trying to stand but was having difficulty. She went to help, but Jordan waved her off impatiently.

"Cane," she said. Ash looked around the room but didn't see it anywhere. After a moment, Jordan sighed and pointed toward the closet. Once Jordan had it in her hand, she got up on her own, but Ash stood close by because she was unsteady on her feet. "Beer."

"I thought you wanted coffee," Ash said impatiently. She had a low tolerance for drunks. They were at best argumentative, and at worst violent. She'd dealt with more of them than she ever wanted to when she'd been a beat cop in LA.

"Right. Coffee. And food." Jordan nodded. "And beer."

Ash called room service and ordered a sandwich for Jordan. When she hung the phone up and turned to face Jordan, she sucked in a breath at the naked woman before her.

"What are you doing?"

"Getting ready for bed." Jordan was still slurring her words and was obviously having trouble standing, but she was determined. Ash was sure Jordan would never remember any of this in the morning.

Ash knew she was staring, and on some level she was aware of the struggle Jordan was having getting her shorts on, but she felt as if she were frozen in place. Jordan looked even better now than she had when she was twenty-eight. How was that even possible?

"Help?" Jordan's plea got Ash moving again. Jordan pulled her shorts up while Ash got the T-shirt ready to pull down over her head. When they were done Ash helped her to the table in the corner before getting her a cup of coffee.

Neither of them spoke. Jordan was obviously trying hard to concentrate on getting the coffee into her mouth rather than dumping it down the front of her shirt. Ash couldn't stop thinking about the medication in the bathroom. She knew more about MS than she had before meeting Maria, but she still didn't know nearly enough.

When Jordan finally finished eating her sandwich and drinking two cups of black coffee, Ash helped her get into bed and turned out the bedside lamp. She turned to go, but Jordan grabbed her wrist firmly.

"Stay."

"I can't, Jordan. I need to go home and get some sleep. I'll check on you in the morning though. Make sure you're up and ready for your tournament."

"Shit, that's tomorrow?"

"Afraid so." Ash looked at the hand still gripping her wrist. For half a second she seriously considered taking her clothes off and crawling into the bed with Jordan. But she knew how stupid that would be. And how desperate it would make her look, taking advantage of Jordan while she was too drunk to seriously consent. Ash didn't want her like that. If they were going to rekindle their relationship, Jordan needed to say she wanted her while actually being sober enough to know what she was saying. As she stood there contemplating what to do, the grip on her wrist slowly loosened until Jordan's hand finally fell away and she was snoring softly.

Without giving too much thought to what she was doing, Ash took a pillow from the other side of the bed and curled up on the couch. She could sleep here just as easily as she could at home, because what if Jordan woke up in the middle of the night and needed something? And if she was being honest with herself, she didn't want to leave her alone.

Chapter Sixteen

Jordan opened her eyes cautiously the next morning, not sure where she was or how she'd gotten there. Or who she was with. She half expected a warm body to be pressed against her, but she was alone. She breathed out a sigh of relief. It was always awkward to wake up with a woman and have to admit to her you didn't remember her name. Thankfully, she'd been in her twenties the last time that happened—the last time she'd been so plastered.

She turned over and realized she was in her own hotel room. She sat up quickly and did her best to ignore the pounding in her head. How the hell had she gotten back to the hotel? The last thing she remembered was the bartender asking her where she was staying.

No, wait, she recalled Ash being there. Standing next to the bed. Or was that merely wishful thinking? When the headache finally subsided to a dull roar, she heard the shower running. This was not good.

"Damn it, Stryker, this is one of the reasons you don't drink so fucking much anymore." She got up and went to the bathroom door, hesitating only slightly before opening it and walking right in. It was her hotel room after all. She opened her mouth to say something but realized she didn't have a clue what to say, so she shook her head and turned toward the sink.

She gripped the edge of the counter and hung her head, but before she could focus on her embarrassment, she saw the box of her medication under a towel. A towel she was pretty sure she hadn't put there.

She grabbed the box and put it in the drawer she should have put it in the night before when she was finished with it. But damn it, who knew she'd come back to her room drunk out of her mind, and apparently with company?

"Do you mind if I brush my teeth?" she asked, raising her voice to be heard over the shower.

"Go ahead."

"Ash?" she asked, turning to face the shower. She heard Ash laugh at the surprise she knew was obvious in her tone.

"Who did you think I was?" Ash asked, pulling back the shower curtain just enough to stick her head out. Her expression turned dark. "Wait, don't answer that."

"What are you doing here?"

"I stayed the night."

"You what?" Jordan felt lightheaded all of a sudden. A fuzzy memory of asking Ash to stay was tickling her brain. Had they slept together? She had on her T-shirt and shorts, which would indicate they hadn't been intimate, but then again, she had absolutely no recall of getting out of her clothes and into these. She sat down hard on the toilet, thankful the cover was down. "Ash, did we…"

She couldn't bring herself to ask. And evidently Ash was going to make her sweat it out because she didn't answer right away. Instead, she finished her shower and reached out to grab a towel that she wrapped around her body before pulling back the curtain and stepping out.

"Did we what?" she asked, looking like she was enjoying Jordan's discomfort a little too much. She grabbed another towel and started drying her hair but her gaze never left Jordan's.

It was strangely intimate being in the bathroom with Ash as she finished her shower. They'd done it many times during their affair, but this somehow felt different to Jordan. Back then it had almost felt like a game, like they were playing at being a couple. This time it felt...*real*. Like this was exactly where she was supposed to be, and Ash was the one she was meant to be with.

But that just didn't make sense. And it wasn't possible. Jordan saw Ash look past her to where the box of medication had been. Jordan decided to not say anything about it. Ash already knew there was something wrong with her, but what were the chances she knew what the meds were for? Jordan really didn't want to talk about it, and that was the main reason something between them just wasn't possible.

She stood and took a step toward Ash, her eyes drawn to the flush on Ash's neck and chest. She stopped when Ash shook her head and placed a hand firmly on her chest, right above Jordan's breast.

"No, we didn't sleep together. I spent the night on the couch because you asked me to stay and it seemed the safest option at the time. And if I'm reading that look in your eye correctly, don't even think about it until you've brushed your teeth."

Jordan smiled. And she felt a small part of her defenses weakening. Maybe if she told herself it was only for whatever time she was in Vegas, it wouldn't hurt so much when she left. But right now, standing in the bathroom with Ash, she knew she was losing the fight to keep her distance. And she was tired of trying. She grabbed her toothbrush and met Ash's eyes in the mirror.

"Would you order breakfast for us?" she asked.

"I already did. It should be here in a few minutes. Large pot of coffee and lots of toast."

"I'm going to jump in the shower. You'll still be here when I get out?"

"If you want me to be."

"I do."

Ash nodded and left the room with her clothes in hand. Jordan looked at herself and took a deep breath. This was a mistake, and deep down she knew it. But she never could say no to Ash. When Ash suggested the previous morning they just have fun together while Jordan was in town, Jordan knew she'd agree to it even as she told herself leaving her again would likely kill her. Yes, it was probably a mistake to play with this particular fire, but Jordan still loved Ash. The realization of that fact, while not completely out of the blue, still surprised her.

❖

Ash didn't take the time to think about why she'd agreed to stay. She quickly dried off and got dressed before the food arrived. She really wanted to go home and do some research on interferon and MS. Maybe she could talk to Maria, who would be able to give her more insight into the disease than any impersonal articles she might find on the Web could possibly provide.

She poured herself a cup of coffee and took it with her to the windows overlooking the strip. She didn't often get to see the view from here, and it was much more impressive at night, but it was still incredible in the light of day. She hadn't really taken the time to look at it the night before, but she hoped she'd be getting another opportunity soon.

"Beautiful, isn't it?" Jordan asked.

Ash turned to look at her and noticed she was limping. Her gaze went to Jordan's leg and she felt a lump forming in her throat. She hated what this disease had done to Maria, and she hated it even more for finding Jordan. When she raised her eyes back to Jordan's face she felt her cheeks flush at having been caught staring.

"Yes, it is beautiful," she answered, not knowing what else to say.

"I was talking about the view," Jordan said, giving her a lopsided grin. She tossed the wet towel she was using to dry her hair onto the foot of the bed and walked to stand next to Ash. "Why did you leave the LAPD?"

Ash stared out the window because it was infinitely safer than looking at Jordan dressed in a purple polo shirt that fit like a glove. And the jean shorts that threatened to leave Ash's mouth watering because of how they fit Jordan's ass. She hadn't told anyone the real reasons behind her leaving LA, but she knew she wouldn't hesitate to tell Jordan. She took a deep breath and cleared her mind, wondering why Jordan hadn't asked about that the other night.

"After you left, Kevin and I tried to have a baby, but it just wasn't working. After a couple of years, we had some tests done and found out he had a low sperm count. There were methods he and the doctors wanted to try, but by then I knew in my heart I wasn't happy with him. That I could never be happy with any man. I'd gotten to the point where I hated even the thought of having sex with him."

"I ruined you."

Ash looked at Jordan and smiled at the cocky grin she had. Ash nodded. Jordan had ruined her, but not only for Kevin.

"Yes, you did," she said quietly. "Not just for men, but apparently for any other women as well. I had a couple affairs with female officers a few years after you, but nothing ever felt right to me. Nobody could measure up, and nobody could fill me with excitement like you could. Then he and his buddies started harassing me at work. They made it a living hell for me there. I didn't really have a choice but to leave."

Ash paused, half expecting Jordan to interject with some smartass response, but Jordan was staring out the window with what looked like sadness in her eyes. Ash waited, but Jordan refused to even look at her.

"If I could go back and change anything in my past, it would be to not panic when you told me you loved me." Ash looked away when Jordan turned her head toward her. "I loved you too, but I was too terrified to admit it. Even to myself. I tried to call you once about three years after you left, but they told me you'd transferred to the East Coast. I took that as a sign I needed to just forget you and move on."

"I wish you would have tried harder to get in touch with me." Jordan's voice sounded strained, and Ash worried for a moment she might cry.

"How different would our lives have been if I'd only admitted my feelings for you then?"

Ash watched helplessly as Jordan turned away and walked to the room service table to pour herself a cup of coffee.

"There are some things that would have happened no matter what, so playing that game is nonproductive," Jordan said with her back to Ash.

Ash felt her heart constrict as it suddenly hit her—this was real. Jordan really had a potentially debilitating disease and it was keeping her from allowing Ash inside. She had to leave. No matter how flirty and suggestive they'd been in the bathroom earlier, it was obvious Jordan had shut herself off again.

"What time will you be done playing tonight?" Ash asked. She set her coffee cup on the table as she walked toward the door.

"I'm not sure. With the breaks, I'm thinking between midnight and one in the morning. If I make it through the day, that is."

"When I get off, I'll go to Starbucks and wait for you. If you don't show up, I won't bother you again." Ash waited, but there was no response, and Jordan again refused to look at her. "Good luck today."

Jordan closed her eyes when the door shut behind Ash and felt a tear run down her cheek. She wanted to scream. How the hell could she act like none of it mattered when all she wanted to do was kiss her? To tear Ash's clothes off and make love to her? To spend the rest of her nights in Vegas wrapped in her arms? She put the coffee cup down before she lost control and hurled it against the wall.

How would their lives have been different if Ash had admitted to Jordan how she felt? They would have been together when Jordan received her diagnosis. Then what? Would she have stayed because she loved her, or because she felt she had to? And how was that choice any different from the one facing them now?

It wasn't, she admitted reluctantly. But there was no way she was going to force Ash to make a decision like that. When her tournament was done for the day, she'd avoid Starbucks and come right back up to her room. Better to stay away from her than to give her the wrong idea.

That settled, she got more coffee and ate some toast in an attempt to squelch the lingering effects of the hangover she had. And the butterflies in her stomach, which she was certain had absolutely nothing to do with the upcoming poker tournament.

CHAPTER SEVENTEEN

Jordan chose to spend her ninety-minute dinner break in the steak house located off the casino floor. She'd taken a seat at the bar and ordered a beer and a nice juicy rib eye cooked medium rare. They were through with six levels of the eleven they were to play on day one, and Jordan was sitting comfortable, up over twenty-five thousand dollars in chips. For the thousand dollar buy-in she'd had to pay, she got three thousand dollars in chips to play with, the same as everyone else.

She'd taken three players out on the first hand of the day. It amazed her how many people wanted to go all in right off the bat. It always seemed like there was at least one at every table. She'd had pocket aces, and there was no way she was going to let some idiot scare her off the bet. She'd taken a risk, sure, because there was never a guarantee pocket aces would hold up, but it was a calculated risk that had paid off. And those three people were out a grand each for about thirty seconds of play.

She was about to take her first bite of her mouthwatering steak when someone took the barstool next to her and bumped her elbow.

"Oh, my God, I'm so sorry!" the woman said as she placed a hand on Jordan's forearm. Jordan put her fork down and turned in her seat.

"It's okay," she said with a smile. She noticed the woman was dressed in the same clothes Ash wore to work, and her nametag declared she was a Rio casino employee named Jan.

"You're Jordan, right?"

"Do I know you?" Jordan's heart rate sped up a bit. Jan didn't look familiar to her.

"We met briefly at the bar last night. We chatted for a bit before you told me you couldn't dance with me because you were in love with someone else."

"I said that?"

"You did. Why? Is it not true?"

How the hell did she answer this question? Yes, it was true, but there was no future for her and Ash. But on the other hand, her libido seemed to have gone on a vacation of its own except where Ash was concerned. Here she was sitting close— very close—to an incredibly attractive young woman, and there was nothing. She didn't understand it.

"It is true, but I'm sorry to admit I don't remember very much about last night. From what I understand, it wasn't my finest hour." Jordan thought maybe she did remember snippets of a conversation with this blond-haired blue-eyed beauty, but the meaning of it all remained just out of her reach. She looked away quickly when she recalled pushing Jan's hand away from her crotch as said hand slowly moved up the inside of her thigh.

"If you change your mind, I'll be there again tonight."

"Thanks, but I don't think so."

"Are you sure?" Jordan stiffened when she felt Jan's hand brush hers on top of the bar.

"Look, I may have been hammered last night, but apparently I knew what I was talking about. I'm not available, and I'm not interested, all right?"

"Fine. Sorry I bothered you." Jan got up and walked away, and Jordan found herself looking over her shoulder at the way her hips swayed.

Absolutely nothing. She couldn't understand it. Normally, when a woman came on to her, they made arrangements to hook up. It was alarming to think she might be losing her sex drive. No, that couldn't be true, because her body had a very real reaction to Ash getting out of the shower that morning. She shook her head and concentrated on her dinner once again.

❖

Jordan was up close to forty-five thousand at the end of the first day. She walked toward the elevators, intent on not even looking toward Starbucks, but then the strangest thing happened. Her feet stopped listening to the orders her brain was giving and she found herself walking toward the table where Ash was waiting for her.

"Hi," Ash said, smiling shyly. "I didn't think you'd come."

"Neither did I, to be perfectly honest," Jordan told her. She sat down without ordering anything and stared at her hands.

"How did you do today?"

"Good. It was a good day." Jordan was so busy studying her hands she almost jumped out of her seat when the barista set a small cup in front of her. She shook her head and looked at the young woman. "I didn't—"

"I ordered it," Ash said as she dismissed the barista.

"You didn't even think I'd show up."

"I asked her to bring it over if she saw someone sit down at the table with me."

Jordan nodded before removing the lid from the cup to let the coffee cool a bit. She had no desire to burn her lips, tongue, and mouth at this hour of the morning. Or any hour of any day, for that matter.

"Thank you," she said after a moment.

"You're welcome."

"So, why are we here?" Jordan didn't like her tone, but for some reason she resented the fact she was sitting there having a cup of coffee with Ash at nearly one o'clock in the morning. She should have been sleeping, resting for another full day of poker, not drinking coffee and sounding like she was pissed off at the world because of it.

"I said I wouldn't bother you anymore if you didn't show up," Ash said. "But here you are, so maybe you should be telling me why we're here."

"I didn't intend to come here," Jordan said with a firm shake of her head. "I was going to go straight up to my room and go to bed."

"You don't sound happy that you're here."

"Damn it, I'm not." Jordan pushed the cup away from her but pulled her hand back quickly when the coffee spilled over and burned her hand. Ash jumped up and hurried to the counter to grab a handful of napkins. Jordan mumbled a thanks as she took them from her and held them to her hand.

"Then why are you here, since you're making it painfully obvious you don't want to be." Ash settled in her chair again and met Jordan's eyes.

"Because you want another fling with me, and despite the fact that you ripped my heart out and stomped all over it fifteen years ago, I can't seem to say no to you."

"But you want to say no?"

"Yes," Jordan answered quickly, but then she shook her head. "No. I don't know what I want. You are the only woman I've ever met who has the ability to completely wreck me."

Ash was silent. She didn't know what to say. She had no intention of pushing Jordan into doing anything. But the way they'd been yesterday morning at her house convinced her Jordan did want her. She had a suspicion the biggest reason Jordan was holding back was because of the MS. Ash had promised herself she would let Jordan be the one to bring it up, so she took a deep breath and set her empty cup aside.

"I didn't force you to come here tonight, Jordan, and for the record, I don't want a fling with you. We were good together, and I know we could be again. I only suggested a fling because of your *complicated* situation for whatever reason you refuse to talk to me about. I just want you so much I would agree to a fling if it was all you were willing to offer." Ash stood and pushed her chair in. "I'm not trying to be overly aggressive, so I'm going home now. You have my number. But remember this—you're the one who suggested we take Maria to the Grand Canyon on Friday, so don't you dare back out on that."

"I'll be there. Don't worry about it."

Ash stared at her for a moment before nodding once and walking away. She was in her car before she finally allowed the ache in her chest to consume her. She knew she had no right to expect Jordan to forgive her for breaking her heart, but that didn't make it hurt any less when Jordan rejected her.

She let the tears fall until they finally stopped on their own before she turned the key in the ignition. When she'd arrived home that morning she'd fallen into bed and slept until it was time to get ready for work. Tonight she planned to do some online research about multiple sclerosis and interferon.

Chapter Eighteen

Ash stayed up until after four in the morning searching the Internet for anything she could find pertaining to MS. She'd visited so many websites and followed so many links, she couldn't remember what information she'd gotten from where. And for God's sake, who knew there were so many different forms of MS? But the general consensus seemed to be that the disease affected everyone differently—no two people had the exact same symptoms. And interferon had been proven to be successful in slowing the progression of MS.

She woke up to the sound of Trixie purring in her ear and she looked at the clock with a groan. Eight thirty. She tried to go back to sleep, but her mind wouldn't stop thinking about Jordan. It bothered her Jordan had been so angry the night before. The Jordan she knew was always happy and took everything in stride. But one of the myriad symptoms she'd discovered had been irritability. Who could blame her though? Ash would be angry as hell if she found out she had a disease like MS. No doubt it had to take its toll.

After finally admitting to herself she wasn't going to be able to sleep any longer, she got up and showered. She fed Trixie before eating a bowl of cereal and deciding today would be as good a day as any to talk to Maria. She quickly washed her breakfast dishes before grabbing the phone and dialing.

"Hello," Maria said after answering on the second ring.

"Good morning. I didn't wake you, did I?"

"Are you kidding?" Maria laughed. "I can't remember the last time I slept past seven. You, on the other hand, rarely get up before noon. What's wrong?"

"I was wondering if I could come over and pick your brain about MS."

"Okay." Maria dragged the word out. "Come on over."

"Thanks," Ash said. She hung up and grabbed her house keys before hurrying next door.

Once settled in at the kitchen table with a cup of coffee in front of her, Ash wasn't even sure where to start. She ran a finger absently around the rim of her mug and tried to gather her thoughts.

"Why the sudden interest in MS?" Marie asked after a few moments of rather awkward silence.

"No reason," she lied. "I just realized I don't know much about it."

"Bullshit." Maria laughed. "Is this about Jordan?"

"What? No, it has nothing to do with her."

"Double bullshit. MS isn't something most people just suddenly decide they want to learn more about. There's usually a reason for wanting information."

Ash thought about lying again, but Maria was right. She hadn't wanted to bring up Jordan's name because she knew Jordan wouldn't want anyone to know. Hell, she hadn't even told Ash yet. It seemed like an invasion of her privacy. But she knew Maria well enough to know she wouldn't say anything about this to anyone, especially Jordan.

"I hadn't seen her in fifteen years before this past week. She has a cane she doesn't use all the time, but it's obvious she has trouble walking and getting up from a seated position sometimes. I've asked her about it, but she says it's muscle spasms."

"And from this you've concluded she has MS?"

"No, in fact, it never even crossed my mind. Not until the other day when I saw a box of interferon and an auto-injector on her bathroom counter." Ash saw Maria's expression change from skepticism to concern in a heartbeat. "I know it's what you take. Is there anything else that drug is used for?"

"Not that I know of," Maria said with a shake of her head. "You know, she probably wasn't lying to you when she said it was muscle spasms. It is a symptom, and it's one of the reasons I have to use the wheelchair. Does she know you saw the medication?"

"I don't know. Neither one of us has said anything about it. She did put it away in a drawer as soon as she realized it was sitting out though, so I would have to assume she suspects I saw it. But I doubt she realizes I know what it's used for." Ash sighed and shook her head. "I don't know if I should bring it up or wait until she does. But then again, I'm worried she won't."

"She needs to be the one to tell you, honey," Maria said as she reached across the table and placed a hand on Ash's forearm. "How long were you two having your affair?"

"Just over three months. Kevin was working undercover so he was never home. It made it rather easy for me to go to Jordan's hotel whenever I wanted with little risk of ever getting caught." But it hadn't stopped her feelings of guilt for cheating on him. He'd deserved better.

"She fell in love with you?" Maria asked and Ash nodded her response. "And you loved her too, right?"

"Sometime during those months I found myself falling in love, yes," she answered. "And it scared the hell out of me."

"Do you still love her?"

"Yes," Ash said without hesitation. "I told her that the other night. I can see in the way she looks at me she still has feelings for me, but she refuses let me in."

"Maybe because you broke her heart? But you think it's because of the MS." A statement, not a question, but Ash nodded. "It makes sense. When someone is diagnosed, it has a tendency to derail your life. My guess is she doesn't know what to expect in the future, so she wants to keep everyone at arm's length. Trust me, if I'd met Lance *after* my diagnosis, I would have done the same thing. Luckily, we were already married and he told me in no uncertain terms he wasn't going anywhere. I really hit the jackpot when I found him."

"Does everyone who has MS end up in a wheelchair?" Ash looked down at her coffee as she spoke the words, finally putting voice to the thing that frightened her the most about it.

"No. There are different forms of the disease, and everyone is affected by it differently. There's a woman in my support group who's in a wheelchair and can't do a thing for herself. She can't feed herself, and she can't speak words so anyone can understand her. She was diagnosed fifteen years ago. Then there's a woman who sees the same neurologist I do who's had it for twenty years and she does fine with a cane. I think that's the scariest thing about MS. You never know what it's going to do to you." Maria leaned back in her chair and gave her a weak smile. "Unfortunately there's no cure for it, so the best any of us can do is take the interferon and hope it does what it's supposed to do. If I hadn't been taking it all along, I might have been where I am now seven or eight years ago."

Ash nodded. Maria was telling her pretty much the same things she'd read on the Internet the night before. It made her feel better hearing it from someone she knew though. It wasn't going to be easy, but she would wait for Jordan to bring it up. Or maybe it would be easy since she'd decided she was going to stay away from her. Ash had put her heart on the line, and what happened next was up to Jordan.

❖

Jordan felt out of sorts all day. She managed to make it through the tournament and had a solid lead over most of the remaining players going into the third and final day of play. She'd expected to see Ash at some point during the day, but she never did. She checked her phone numerous times, but there were no texts, and no missed calls. She'd thought about calling her during the dinner break, but ultimately decided not to. It worried her to realize she longed to hear Ash's voice. It had only been a few days, but she missed knowing she would see her at some point.

She shook her head as she left the poker room and headed for the elevators. At the last second she veered off and walked into Starbucks, hoping maybe Ash would be there again, waiting for her.

She wasn't, and Jordan felt her heart drop.

"Hello again," came a voice from behind her. She turned to see Jan smiling.

"Hi," Jordan said as she walked past, headed for the elevators again. She stopped abruptly and faced her again. Jan worked here. Probably with Ash, if the way she was dressed both now and the previous night was any indication. She couldn't help herself. "Is Ashley Noble working today?"

"Today as in Tuesday, or today as in Monday?"

Jordan pulled her phone out of her pocket and saw it was after midnight. "Either. Both. Is she here?"

"She got off at twelve. She'll be back at three thirty this afternoon." Jan smiled, but it wasn't seductive as it had been before. Jordan breathed a sigh of relief. Maybe she'd finally gotten the message that she wasn't interested. "Should I tell her you were asking about her?"

"No," she answered quickly. "I'm sure I'll run into her sometime."

Jordan walked as quickly as she could to the elevators. She fought the urge to call Ash when she got to her room and instead took a quick shower before falling into bed. She fell asleep with images of Ash running through her mind.

CHAPTER NINETEEN

Jordan's heart was pounding. She readjusted the Phillies baseball hat she was wearing and felt the sweat under the band. She was one of only four players left at the final table, but she didn't have the most chips. Not that it really mattered since Paul, the player who did have the most chips, was playing recklessly. It seemed to Jordan he was desperate and just trying to get the other three to fold so he could take the blinds every hand.

Jordan hadn't had a good enough hand to feel comfortable calling his bet, but this hand was looking better. She had ace queen suited. Paul pushed his entire stack in without hesitation. The other two players folded, but Jordan didn't do anything right away. She looked at her cards again as if she were trying to decide what to do. She shook her head and acted like she was going to fold, but then changed her mind.

"What the hell?" she said with a shrug before pushing her chips in. If she lost, she'd be done. If she won, she'd be over two million in chips. Unfortunately, Paul's stack was bigger than hers, so he'd still be in it no matter what the outcome of this hand was.

Paul smiled, looking confident as he turned his cards over. King queen offsuit. The smile faded when Jordan revealed her cards. She stood and stretched her back as she waited for the dealer to reveal the flop.

The flop was good to Jordan. Two queens and a ten. The turn was a king, giving Paul a full boat, queens over kings. The only card that could win it for Jordan was an ace. She closed her eyes for the river. Paul's shouted expletive told Jordan all she needed to know. She opened her eyes and saw an ace on the table.

She smiled as the dealer pushed the chips in her direction, the first show of any emotion from her in the entire tournament. She started to believe she had a real shot at winning this thing. Almost eighteen hundred people had entered the tourney, and she was one of only four left. Maybe three, because Paul was looking even more desperate now. He had a million in chips left, but Jordan had a feeling he was going to do something stupid. Anxiety wasn't an emotion that would serve you well at the poker table.

Just as Jordan thought, Paul went all in on the next hand and lost. She took a deep breath and tried to calm her nerves. She looked around the room, noticing the spectator area had thinned out a bit. She'd been watching for Ash, but hadn't seen her in the room at all yesterday or today. She shook her head and turned her focus to the table. Hoping Ash would show up was going to cost her this tournament and its three hundred thousand dollar grand prize. She needed to get her head in the game.

The next hand saw another player eliminated. It was down to her and a guy named Chris. He met her eyes from across the table and nodded once. She returned the gesture.

"You're good. Why haven't I seen you before?" he asked while the dealer was shuffling the cards.

"This is my first big tourney," she answered.

"Really," he said, making it sound as though he thought she was full of shit. "You play Internet poker?"

"Some." She shrugged. She really hated talking while she was playing. Up until now, Chris had been quiet. Why was he being so chatty now? He was probably trying to throw her off her game. "Good luck."

"You too."

Thankfully, he shut up when the hole cards were dealt. He had the first big blind and Jordan's cards were shit. She folded. He did the same on the next hand. They had twelve consecutive hands where neither of them bid past the blind. Then Jordan finally got cards worth taking a risk on. Pocket kings. She raised before the flop and Chris looked at her warily. He probably thought she was tired of the cat-and-mouse game and was finally trying to get something going. He thought she was bluffing.

After the flop Jordan checked. The cards were ten jack queen, all hearts. Jordan had the king of hearts in her hand. She concentrated hard on controlling her breathing because she really didn't want to give away how good her hand was. The ace of hearts would give her a royal flush. The nine would give her a straight flush. Any other heart would give her a king high flush. The first two possibilities were impossible to beat.

Chris bet big, but didn't go all in, which told Jordan he probably didn't have anything better than a pair based solely on how he'd bet previous hands. He could have a flush, which at this point could be devastating to her. She doubted it though, so she went all in. He took a long time contemplating whether he should call her bet. He stared at her for a few minutes, trying to read anything he could from her facial expressions. She kept neutral and leaned back in her chair like she was bored waiting for him to decide.

He finally pushed all his chips in, which was a shorter stack than her own, meaning if she won the hand, she'd win the tournament. If she lost the hand, she'd be down a considerable amount. He flipped his cards over to reveal pocket queens, giving him three of a kind. Jordan needed a heart—any heart—or an ace in order to pull it out. They were both standing, Chris with his hands behind his head and Jordan gripping the back of her chair thinking *heart heart heart.*

The turn was a three of clubs, which didn't help either of them. Jordan waited, sweat rolling down her back, for the river. She decided instead of watching the dealer reveal the river card, she would watch Chris. His reaction would tell her everything she needed to know about whether she'd won or lost.

When the card was dealt, Chris dropped his arms to his side and hung his head in obvious disbelief. "Damn it!"

Jordan glanced down and saw the four of hearts on the table. She smiled to herself and waved to the crowd as they cheered her victory. She was careful not to celebrate her win too much because all it would do is show the other players she liked to rub it in. If she did that, they'd be gunning for her next time.

"Great game, Stryker," Chris said as he extended a hand.

"Thanks, you too," she said, gripping his hand briefly.

"Congratulations," the dealer said as he stood and left the table.

"Can I buy you a drink?" Chris asked. Jordan studied his face, trying to see if he was trying to pick her up, but she didn't get that vibe from him.

"Sure," she said with a nod. She scanned the room to see if Ash had slipped in sometime during the final hands, but she wasn't there. Jordan sighed. It surprised her to realize how much she wanted to celebrate this win with her.

❖

"Did you hear?" Oz asked as he walked into Ash's office. It was a little after eight in the evening, and Ash was surprised to see him. He'd worked that morning, and it wasn't like him to hang around after his shift. She dropped her pen and decided she could finish paperwork later. Oz obviously had something to tell her.

"Did I hear what?"

"Jordan Stryker won the no-limit hold 'em tournament." Oz smiled, obviously pleased with himself because he knew something she didn't.

"That's great." Ash tried not to sound too excited about it, but it was a big deal. There was a lot of money in those tournaments. She forced herself to not grab her cell phone and call to congratulate her. At this point it was up to Jordan to make the next move.

"Really? *That's great*? That's all you can say?"

"What do you want me to say, Oz?" Ash sighed and looked down at her paperwork.

"What's going on? I thought you two were working on being friends with possible benefits. Has something changed you haven't told me about?"

"Believe it or not, I don't tell you everything."

"Yes, you do," he said with a grin. "Because I'm the best straight male friend you have. And you do better with women than I do, which is why you so enjoy telling me everything."

"To rub it in?" Ash laughed as he gave her an exaggerated nod.

"Exactly. So tell me what happened."

Ash stared at him for a moment, wondering if she should tell him, while at the same time knowing she would sooner or later. So why not do it now and get it out of the way? He'd never judged her, and perhaps he'd have some insight she was lacking.

"I told her I loved her."

"Then or now?"

"Now. Fuck, Oz, I think I scared her away."

"Bullshit. She said she loved you, right? That's why you ended it with her?" Ash nodded her response. "So I doubt you saying it now would scare her away. Something else has to be going on."

"I think it has to do with why she uses a cane."

"Did you ask her about it?"

"She won't give me a straight answer." Ash held her hands up to indicate she had no idea where to go with Jordan. There was no way she was going to tell him about the MS. She knew he wouldn't say anything to anyone about it, but she'd already told Maria, and she didn't feel right telling more people. "But I think it's something serious and she's trying to protect me from it."

"Maybe she's trying to protect herself," he said.

"How so?"

"Perhaps it is something serious, and when she's told people in the past they've dumped her. I can only imagine the fear she might have at being rejected by you again, especially if she's still in love with you."

It wasn't like Ash hadn't considered the possibility, but hearing someone else put voice to that particular worry made it seem even more likely. But the crux of the problem remained. How could she get Jordan to trust her with the news of the MS, and what would she have to do to make Jordan believe she wouldn't reject her again?

CHAPTER TWENTY

By Thursday night Jordan still hadn't run into Ash, nor had she given in and called her. She knew she'd have to call to find out what time they were leaving for the Grand Canyon in the morning, but on some level she was dreading talking to her. She waited until almost ten o'clock to call, telling herself it was so there would be no excuse for them to get together that night. In reality, she'd wanted to call earlier and invite her to dinner. Not being with Ash was starting to hurt even more than it had when she'd left LA.

"Hey, Jordan," Ash said when she answered the phone.

"Hi. I'm calling to find out when I should be at your place in the morning. We're still going to the Grand Canyon, right?"

"Yeah. I'd like to leave as early as possible," Ash said. "Can you be here at six?"

"Jesus, are you trying to kill me?"

"Not a morning person?" Ash laughed and Jordan felt the warmth of it in her gut.

"Not in the least. Especially after being up until after midnight almost every night this week," Jordan said. It felt good to be able to talk to Ash without it being awkward. It occurred to her she hadn't spoken to Ash since the tournament ended. "I won, by the way."

"I know. I saw the list," Ash said, her voice getting softer. "I wanted to congratulate you, but I said I wouldn't call."

"You could have."

"So could you."

"I was afraid to." Jordan closed her eyes, not believing she'd just said those words out loud. On the other hand, it was true, so why not tell her?

"Afraid of me?" Ash sounded genuinely surprised.

"Afraid of *me*," Jordan answered after a moment. "Afraid of the things you make me feel. Things I swore I'd never feel again. For anyone."

"You don't have to be afraid."

"Yes, I do." Jordan ran a hand through her hair and fell back onto the bed. "Ash, I could so easily start things up with you again, but trust me when I say it would be a bad idea."

"Why?"

Jordan thought about it for a minute. She seriously considered telling Ash about the MS, but what good would it do in the long run? Because no matter what, there could never be anything lasting between them. She didn't want anyone's pity. Pity was what she felt when her father was diagnosed with cancer. Pity was what she felt when her mother was diagnosed with dementia and put into a nursing home. Pity wasn't something she ever wanted anyone to feel for her.

"What part of trust me didn't you get?"

"I do trust you, Jordan. But trust goes both ways."

"What do you mean?" Jordan sat up, her heart racing. She'd begun to think maybe Ash hadn't seen the medication on the counter the morning she was there, but her words made her wonder. She'd have said something, wouldn't she? The fact she wasn't answering right away caused Jordan's defenses to go up. "Ash, what do you mean?"

"Nothing. I just want you to trust me too."

"I do. I always have." She was still worried, but Ash's tone calmed her a little.

"Come over. If you stay here tonight I'll make sure you're up and ready to go by six."

Jordan laughed, and she heard Ash doing the same on her end.

"I have a feeling if I stayed there tonight, we'd still be up at six tomorrow morning."

"Now there's a thought."

"Good night, Ash. I'll be there bright and early."

"I'll have a cup of coffee waiting for you."

Ash hung up without saying good-bye. She hadn't really expected Jordan to take her up on the offer, but she'd hoped for a moment she would. Maybe when they returned from the Grand Canyon tomorrow. Maria had already told her she was going to bail on them for dinner again so they could have some time alone to talk. She just hoped Jordan really could trust her enough to confide in her about her medical situation.

All of the unknown elements of it scared Ash, and she was sure Jordan was scared as well. But Ash knew what she wanted, and losing Jordan all over again was definitely not in her plans.

❖

"Good morning, Sunshine," Ash said when she answered the door the next morning.

"Fuck you," Jordan said. Ash laughed at her, but Jordan just glared. "You said you'd have coffee."

"It's ready. Come on in."

Jordan made it as far as the kitchen table before sitting down and holding her head in her hands. Ash nudged her with a cup before sitting across from her.

"You don't have a hangover, do you?"

"No, smart-ass, I do not have a hangover." Ash watched as she took a sip of the coffee and closed her eyes with an appreciative groan. "I'll have you know I went to bed right after we hung up. I wish I could say I went right to sleep, but alas, I think I tossed and turned most of the night."

Ash wanted to ask her why she couldn't get to sleep, and to find out if it was the same reasons she had trouble sleeping. But before she could open her mouth, the front door crashed open and they heard Maria's cheerful voice.

"Rise and shine! Up and at 'em, ladies!" A few seconds later, the wheelchair came through the doorway and Maria looked like she'd been up for hours.

"Are you kidding me?" Jordan asked Ash. "Is she always like this?"

"Pretty much, yeah."

"Come on, get a move on. It's going to take me a while to hike to the bottom of the canyon and back, and I need to be home by eight. My mother called and said she's coming for the weekend."

Ash slapped Jordan on the back when Jordan choked on her coffee. Jordan looked at Maria then to Ash with a worried look on her face.

"She's kidding, right?"

"Yes, she's kidding." Ash assured her, but she couldn't resist a little more teasing. "She knows it would take two days to hike to the bottom and back out again."

"What's the matter, Jordan? You don't like self-deprecating humor from the lady in the wheelchair?" Maria winked at Ash before rolling up to the table and grabbing Ash's cup. "Too bad, because I can do this all day. By the way, I'm serious about having to be back by eight. Mom's flight lands at seven thirty."

"So you're cancelling our dinner plans again?" Ash asked. She looked at Jordan to see her reaction and wasn't disappointed at the small smile she tried to hide.

"Sorry." She shrugged. "I'm sure you two can find something to do without me."

The look Jordan gave her caused Ash to tremble slightly. She couldn't describe it any other way than predatory. Yes, there was no doubt they could figure out something do to. And Ash was pretty sure she knew exactly what Jordan had in mind.

CHAPTER TWENTY-ONE

"You seem a little uneasy around me, Jordan," Maria said while Ash went inside to pay for gas. Jordan turned in the passenger seat as she shook her head and started to protest, but Maria held a hand up to stop her. "I've been in this chair long enough to know when someone is uncomfortable so don't even try to deny it."

Jordan couldn't deny it. When she looked at Maria, all she could see was herself sometime in the future. It was not knowing when she'd end up there that scared her. She struggled to find something to say, because she did like Maria. Jordan didn't want her to think she didn't, but Maria saved her.

"Do you know anyone with MS?"

"Yeah," she answered before she could stop herself.

"Is it someone close to you?"

"You could say that." Jordan hoped the questions wouldn't get any closer to the truth, so she decided to change the track they were on. "How long have you had it?"

"I was diagnosed fifteen years ago, but after learning more about it and what the symptoms are, I'm pretty sure I've had it all my adult life. How about you?"

"What?" Jordan forced a laugh and waved her off. "I don't have it."

"Really? Most women your age don't need a cane to get around. And I've seen the tremors in your hands. And your feet fall asleep more than anyone I've ever known. Have you seen a doctor about it? Have you had any tests done to rule it out?"

Jordan was never so relieved to see Ash as she was then. She decided not answering Maria's questions would be the simplest way out of the situation. She faced forward again as Ash got into the vehicle and fastened her seat belt. Jordan just hoped Maria wouldn't press the issue, especially in front of Ash.

❖

"My God, this is beautiful," Maria said as they stood as close to the rim of the canyon as they could without feeling as though they'd fall over the edge. The awe in her voice was unmistakable, and Jordan found herself smiling. She loved coming here with someone who'd never seen it before. "It doesn't look real. It looks like a painting. A massive, incredibly detailed painting."

"It is amazing," Ash said in agreement.

"I never get tired of it." Jordan said. "I grew up in Phoenix, and when I was little my parents brought my brother and me here a couple of times a year. Most of my friends went to Disneyland or the beach, but we always came here. It was the only time I felt like we were a family. At home, my father was a Marine and was always working, most of the time deployed somewhere or other. And I don't think my mother ever really wanted to have children. She spent as little time as possible with Matt and me."

Jordan jumped slightly when she felt Ash's hand slide into hers, their fingers intertwining as though they'd been doing it forever. She glanced at Ash and saw a sad smile. She squeezed Ash's hand gently and was comforted when Ash returned the gesture.

"Are you close to your parents now?" Maria asked, never taking her eyes from the spectacle of nature before them.

"My father's dead. My mother has dementia, so I guess in a way she doesn't have children, except on the rare occasion when she actually remembers who we are."

"I'm so sorry," Ash said quietly.

"Do you visit her often?" Maria asked.

"No," Jordan said. "My brother's much better about that than I am. I went to see her for her birthday before I came to Vegas though. For the majority of my visit, she kept asking me who the hell I was thinking I could come into a stranger's room and just sit by the bed."

"That must be hard." Maria finally turned her chair to face them and smiled when she saw them holding hands. Jordan tried to pull away, but Ash held tighter.

"Not really. I was never close to either of them, especially after I came out."

"What do you say we get some lunch?" Ash asked, obviously sensing Jordan didn't want to talk about her family anymore. "I could stand here looking at this all day, but I don't want to starve."

❖

They spent the early afternoon trying to explore the village, but most of the time Maria urged them back to the rim where they would stand looking at the canyon in silence. Ash felt more relaxed than she had in years, and it felt undeniably good to be spending time with Jordan.

At three o'clock she gave the bad news they needed to get going if Maria wanted to be home in time for her mother's arrival. After much grumbling about how she'd rather stay right where she was for the rest of her life, Maria finally gave in and allowed Ash to put her and the chair back into the SUV.

Jordan drove them home and Ash took the time to really examine her feelings for Jordan. She knew she loved her; there was no doubt in her mind about that. She assumed Jordan was afraid to get involved because of the MS, but what if there was a different reason? Ash wanted more from her than just a two-week fling, but would she be able to convince Jordan it was what they both wanted? Because she could see it in Jordan's eyes when she looked at her, and it was obvious in the way they'd held hands throughout most of the day. She promised herself she'd do everything in her power over the next fourteen days to convince Jordan they belonged together. Starting with tonight.

Ash glanced into the back seat and saw Maria was sound asleep. She placed her hand tentatively on Jordan's thigh and breathed a sigh of relief when Jordan's hand covered it.

"Will you have dinner with me tonight?" Ash asked.

"Yes," Jordan answered. "Where would you like to go?"

"My place."

Jordan looked at her for a moment before redirecting her gaze to the road in front of her. Ash could tell Jordan was nervous because it was the same look she'd given her the first night they'd slept together. Ash smiled and turned her hand palm up to lace their fingers together again.

"You really think that's a good idea?"

"I think it's the most brilliant idea I've had in forever."
Ash wished she didn't have to have the seat belt on, because
she wanted nothing more than to lie down with her head in
Jordan's lap. "There's beef stew in the slow cooker, and I
bought some garlic bread I just need to heat up. And a nice
bottle of Chianti to go with it."

"Are you trying to seduce me?" Jordan raised an eyebrow
in question and Ash laughed softly so she wouldn't wake
Maria.

"That depends. Is it working?"

"I think it might be. Anything beef is my weakness."

"I remember." Ash turned her head to look out the
window, resting her forehead there. Jordan centered her like
no one else had ever been able to. She was inordinately happy
that they could flirt like this after everything that happened
between them. She never dreamed she'd even see her again,
let alone feel this level of familiarity. She couldn't stop the
smile pulling at the corners of her mouth.

"Hey, wait a minute," Jordan said suddenly. Ash looked at
her, wondering what was wrong. "You said last week that you
take Maria into town on Friday nights for dinner."

"That's right."

"But you had to have had the stew already cooking before
she got there and told you she had to cancel your dinner plans."
Jordan said, feigning hurt by placing a hand over her heart.
"You already knew she wasn't going to dinner with you, and
this was your evil plan all along, wasn't it?"

"Evil? No." Ash went along with Jordan's playful banter.
"Genius, maybe, but not evil. And it was Maria's idea."

"Is her mother really coming for the weekend?"

"Yes, both her parents are. It's their anniversary, and
it's difficult for Maria to travel long distances, so they come

here to celebrate. They live in Massachusetts." Ash studied Jordan's profile for a moment before pulling her hand away. It was getting difficult to keep herself from moving it up higher on Jordan's thigh. "You aren't upset, are you?"

"No, Ash, I'm not." She reached for Ash's hand and Ash let her pull it back into her lap. "And when we get out of this damn car I'll show you how not upset I am. How much farther is it?"

"Less than an hour."

"Christ, I might be dead by then," Jordan muttered.

Ash was surprised when Jordan placed Ash's hand between her legs and pushed it against her center as she pushed back with her hips. She held her own legs together tightly and bit back a groan when she felt a surge of wetness. The answering heat coming from Jordan's center told Ash all she needed to know. The next hour was going to crawl by.

CHAPTER TWENTY-TWO

They made sure Maria was home safe before pulling Ash's SUV into the garage. As soon as the overhead door closed, Ash twisted in her seat and shoved her hand between Jordan's legs again. Jordan grabbed her wrist and shook her head.

"Please," she heard herself beg. She rested her forehead against Jordan's shoulder. "I need you, Jordan. I need to touch you. Now."

"And let the fine meal you spent all day making go to waste?" Jordan smiled. When Ash pulled away, Jordan put a hand behind her neck and held her in place. Ash almost melted at the intensity in Jordan's eyes. "Don't worry. I won't change my mind and bail on you, all right? Besides, for what I have planned for you, we'll both need sustenance."

Ash bit her bottom lip hard to pull her mind from the fact if she moved just right against the seam of her shorts, she'd come right there in the truck without Jordan ever touching her. How embarrassing would that be?

"Do you mind if I take a quick shower while you get dinner ready?" Jordan asked when they were inside the house.

"Go ahead. There's a robe on the back of the bathroom door you can use if you like." Ash forced herself to go into the kitchen and warm up the garlic bread. Every fiber of her being wanted to be in that shower with Jordan.

She tried not to think about Jordan upstairs. In her shower. Naked. Lathering up her body. She bit her lip again but couldn't stifle the groan at the visual she now couldn't get out of her head. When she heard the water shut off a few minutes later, she filled their bowls with stew, and put the bread on a plate before opening the wine and pouring them each a glass.

Her knees almost gave out when Jordan walked into the kitchen, the white robe cinched loosely around her waist, her feet bare, and her hair slicked back. Jordan held a chair out for her, and as soon as she was seated, Jordan pressed her lips to Ash's jaw, right beneath her ear. She was shocked Jordan remembered that was her sensitive spot.

"This looks and smells amazing," Jordan said as she took a seat. After a sip of wine she picked up her spoon and started eating. "Oh, my God, this is wonderful." She leaned forward and pointed at Ash's bowl with her spoon. "You're not eating."

"Can't," Ash managed, her eyes glued to the cleavage exposed by the robe Jordan was wearing. There was very little left to the imagination. "I might choke to death if you keep doing that."

Jordan looked down and grinned before pulling the robe tighter around her chest. Ash was grateful Jordan seemed to have the decency to blush. Ash put a spoonful in her mouth but couldn't taste anything. The only thing she wanted on the menu tonight was sitting in the chair across from her.

"What changed?" Ash asked after they spent a few minutes eating and not talking.

"I'm sorry?"

"You were so adamant about nothing happening between us," Ash explained. She hoped she wasn't making a mistake by pointing out Jordan's former reluctance to what they were apparently about to do. "But since we talked on the phone last night you seem to have done a complete one eighty. Especially now since you seem to be trying to flash me at every opportunity."

Jordan didn't answer right away but merely looked at her food as she pushed it around in the bowl. She finally set her spoon down and pushed the bowl away before leaning back in her seat and meeting Ash's eyes.

"I was an ass to you Sunday night at Starbucks. I felt bad about it, and I was too nervous to call and apologize." Jordan smiled and shook her head. "I lied when I said anything beef is my weakness. You are my only weakness. It isn't your fault that I can't seem to say no to you, and I shouldn't have taken my frustrations out on you. When the tournament was over on Tuesday night, I wanted to go out and celebrate. But then I realized the only woman I wanted to share it with was you. I'm sorry, Ash. Can you forgive me?"

"Of course I forgive you."

"Thank you."

"You won a hell of a lot of money," Ash said with a grin.

"Close to three hundred grand." Jordan nodded. "But that's nothing compared to what I could win in the Main Event. Last year the winner got over eight million."

"When's your first day for that?"

"Not until the third day, which is a week from Monday. Since I entered so late, there weren't any open slots for Saturday or Sunday. I have another no-limit hold 'em tournament starting this Sunday though. Same setup as the other one I played." Jordan stood and held her hand out to Ash, who shook her head.

"I should do the dishes."

"Seriously?" Jordan couldn't help but laugh as she looked around the kitchen. "They'll still be here in the morning, you know."

"You drive a hard bargain." Ash took her hand and Jordan pulled her to her feet. "Why don't you bring the wine upstairs while I hop in the shower?"

Jordan nodded and smiled before watching Ash disappear up the stairs. She took a deep breath and sat down for a minute. Was she doing the right thing, or was she merely setting herself up for another fall? And did it really matter? She knew they were headed for this from the night she'd gone to the show with Ash. She'd be lying if she said she didn't want it. She'd never wanted anything more. But it could only be a fling. And she needed to make sure Ash knew that before it went too far.

With a sigh, she grabbed the bottle of wine and their glasses and went up to the bedroom. By the time she filled them and sat on the edge of the bed, Ash was coming out of the bathroom, covered by a robe of her own.

"Hers and hers robes?" Jordan asked, not liking the pang of jealousy that shot through her chest at the thought. She watched as Ash walked toward her without speaking. The predatory look in Ash's eyes set her body on fire.

"I don't do laundry as often as I should." Ash placed a hand firmly on Jordan's chest and pushed her onto her back as she straddled her. "This way I always have at least one clean robe."

Jordan thought she'd explode when Ash put a hand between their bodies and her fingers slid easily inside her. Ash groaned and Jordan closed her eyes. Her hands cupped Ash's ass and Ash leaned down to capture Jordan's earlobe with her teeth. Jordan's hips thrust involuntarily as a jolt of excitement coursed through her.

"But I'm pretty sure neither one of them are clean anymore." Ash's tongue moved slowly along Jordan's jaw before nipping her chin lightly and moving down her throat. She moved quickly so she was kneeling between Jordan's legs.

"Ash, wait," Jordan managed in a strangled voice as she lifted her head. They needed to set ground rules, didn't they? So in the morning they were on the same page. There was a reason for it, she was certain, but coherent thought escaped her at the moment. All that mattered was the way Ash was touching her.

"Why? You don't want this?" Ash's smile told Jordan she knew damn well she wanted this.

"God, yes, I want it," Jordan said, her head falling back to the mattress. She covered her eyes with her arm as she rested her other hand on her stomach. She felt Ash climb onto the bed and stretch out beside her. She allowed Ash to pull her arm away from her face.

"Jordan, you're scaring me. What's wrong?"

"Nothing." Jordan wiped a tear from the corner of her eye. She'd never cried in front of anyone except her brother, and she wasn't going to start now.

"Bullshit. Please talk to me." Ash put a hand on her cheek and forced her to look at her.

The love and desire she saw in Ash's eyes was nearly her undoing. She forcibly stopped herself from telling Ash about the MS. She tried to turn her head away, just so she could gather her thoughts, but Ash wouldn't allow it, so Jordan put what she hoped looked like a genuine smile on her face.

"It's nothing. This is just a little overwhelming." What Jordan was telling her wasn't a lie; it just wasn't the whole truth. She touched Ash's cheek with the back of her fingers as she spoke. "Ten days ago, I was sure I'd never see you again.

And I really thought I was okay with that. But now, here with you, I feel like I'm really alive again. I don't feel lost anymore. But I didn't know I was lost until now. Does that make any sense?"

"Yes," Ash said with a nod. "It makes perfect sense. I couldn't let myself see it before, but it's all so clear now. I don't know what's going to happen when you're done playing poker, but I'm willing to find out. Are you?"

"Yes." Jordan said even though she knew what would happen. She'd go back to Philly—alone. But that didn't mean she couldn't enjoy herself in the meantime. That they couldn't both enjoy themselves. She stood and let her robe fall to the floor before walking to the other side of the bed and getting under the covers. She watched with a growing fire deep in her core as Ash did the same. When she crawled into the bed, Jordan reached for her and pulled Ash on top of her, spreading her legs so Ash could settle in between her thighs. "Now, where were we?"

Ash smiled as she pushed herself down under the covers. Jordan closed her eyes and arched her back when Ash pushed inside her again. She couldn't stifle the moan when she felt Ash's mouth close around her clit, sucking gently. The fire exploded almost immediately at the base of her spine and worked its way through her body. She threaded her fingers through Ash's hair and held her where she needed her, thrusting against her mouth until she was completely spent.

It seemed like forever, yet not nearly long enough, before her body relaxed back into the mattress and she released her hold on Ash. When she felt her strength returning, she urged Ash back up to lay beside her.

"No one's ever been able to make me come as fast as you can," she said when her breathing finally evened out. She brushed a strand of hair away from Ash's eyes and kissed her, moaning at the taste of her own desire, so incredibly sexy on Ash's lips and tongue. "You always did know exactly what I needed."

"But next time, it will be slower. I want to enjoy every inch of your body tonight." Ash said, giving no resistance when Jordan slowly pushed her onto her back. "Yes, Jordan, I need you so badly. Please, go inside. Don't make me wait."

Jordan held her gaze as she moved her hand down across Ash's stomach and into her wetness. She thought she might come all over again at the look in Ash's eyes when she easily pushed two fingers inside her. They fell into a slow rhythm as Ash moved her hand to the back of Jordan's neck and pulled her closer.

"Don't close your eyes," Jordan said. "I want to see you when you come."

Ash nodded and held onto her as their movements got a little faster and their breathing more erratic. Jordan loved the way Ash's eyes would start to close when her thumb rubbed against her clit with each thrust. Ash held on tighter and Jordan could feel the muscles tightening around her fingers, but she stopped her movements.

"God, no, don't stop now," Ash pleaded, staring into her eyes.

"I'm not nearly ready for this to be over, baby," Jordan told her. "Just relax and let me give you what you need."

"I might explode," she whispered.

"Yes, you will, but not from me stopping."

Ash's pupils got amazingly large right before she crushed her lips against Jordan's. She moaned into Ash's mouth as Ash urged her to thrust her fingers again. Jordan did, and Ash cried out in her mouth as her body clamped down on Jordan's fingers. Ash broke the kiss but kept their foreheads pressed together as her hips kept moving, obviously trying to milk every last tremor she could while Jordan was still inside her.

"Fuck," she said when Jordan slowly pulled out and pressed the heel of her hand against her clit. When Jordan put her fingers in her mouth and sucked her juices off, Ash flipped them over and pressed her center against Jordan's firm thigh. "Fuck."

"We just did," Jordan grinned as she licked her lips. "But I can do this all night. Too bad you have to work tomorrow."

"I don't," Ash said before taking a nipple into her mouth. "I'm off until Sunday because I'll be working nine days straight. So I can do this all night, all day tomorrow, and all of tomorrow night."

"Don't you need to sleep sometime?"

"Sleep's overrated."

CHAPTER TWENTY-THREE

Ash opened her eyes and groaned when she saw the clock said it was seven in the morning. Her mood improved when she felt Jordan press her body tightly against her from behind and put an arm around her middle, holding her in place. She lost count of how many times they'd reached for one another through the night. God knew she should be satisfied, but it seemed she couldn't get enough of Jordan. Or Jordan her. She closed her eyes and pressed her ass back against Jordan, causing Jordan to take in a deep breath.

"Jesus, you are insatiable," Jordan mumbled.

"I could say the same about you."

"Yeah, ain't it grand?"

Ash laughed at the smile she heard in Jordan's voice. She sucked in a breath when Jordan's hand moved to her breast and lightly squeezed her nipple at the same time her mouth moved to that spot right below her ear.

"I think we need to eat something, don't we?" Ash asked, even though leaving the bed was the last thing she wanted to do. She was afraid if they got up the magical bubble would burst and Jordan would remember her objections to them getting involved again.

"I think I'd rather have you for breakfast," Jordan said into her ear. "Food will still be there later."

Ash turned in her arms and forced Jordan onto her back. She straddled her hips and rubbed herself against Jordan's abdomen. She threw her head back when Jordan gripped her hips and forced her to slide a little further down her body.

"You are so fucking sexy," Jordan said, her hands moving slowly up Ash's torso and around to cover her breasts. Ash leaned into her touch and sucked in her bottom lip, not wanting this to end—ever. "So damn beautiful."

"I want your mouth on me, baby," Ash said, feeling uncharacteristically needy. Her sex was so swollen it ached, and she knew Jordan could give her what she needed. Jordan had always been the only one who could.

She watched as Jordan smiled up at her before moving her hands to her ass and urging her forward until she was hovering over Jordan's face. She was close enough to be able to feel Jordan's heated breath on her wet flesh, which ignited her body even more. She cried out when Jordan entered her with her tongue.

"I'm so close, Jordan," she said. Her body tensed and she went over the edge when Jordan swiped her tongue once along her clit and thrust her fingers inside her at the same time. Jordan held her against her mouth as she rode out the waves of pleasure before finally collapsing next to Jordan. "Damn, that was hot."

"That's my idea of breakfast in bed." Jordan kissed her throat and pulled her tighter against her body. "But we should probably eat something a little more substantial."

"You've got to be close too," Ash said as she slid a hand down Jordan's abdomen. They were both sweating from the hours they'd spent pleasuring each other, and her hand moved easily across her skin. "Let me take care of you."

"Later," Jordan said. She framed Ash's face between her hands and kissed her, and Ash felt the answering call of her body when Jordan's tongue slid along hers.

"Fuck," Ash said as she pulled away from her. "You can turn me on with just a kiss. I should be melted into a pool of ecstasy after all the times you made me come since last night. Yet I can't seem to get enough of you."

Jordan looked like she might start to cry, and Ash touched her cheek tenderly.

"I've missed you so much," Jordan said. "It's crazy that I didn't have a clue exactly how much until this past week. I'm afraid to let you go. I just want to stay here in your arms and forget about the rest of the world."

"I'm not going anywhere, baby," Ash assured her. She rested her head on Jordan's chest and allowed the strong, steady heartbeat to comfort her. She was suddenly scared to death that Jordan was going to leave her when she was done playing poker. How could she possibly make Jordan believe she wanted to spend the rest of her life with her?

Jordan stood in the shower letting the water beat down hard and hot against her neck and shoulders. She hurt in places she hadn't hurt for years. Nobody had ever given her a workout like Ash could, and it felt good. Better than good. And Jordan knew that was bad. She turned and lifted her face to the spray, trying not to think about her neurologist telling her that heat would make her symptoms worse. Even the heat from a hot shower. How fucked up was that? Was she supposed to never take a hot shower again?

"I've left a pair of shorts and a T-shirt on the counter for you if you want something to wear other than what you had on yesterday," Ash said, speaking loud enough to be heard over the water. "Are you sure you want to go into town to have breakfast?"

"Have you looked in your refrigerator lately?" Jordan chuckled as she reached down to turn the water off. She opened the door to the shower and accepted the towel Ash held out to her. She held it to her face for a moment and then put it around her shoulders, trying not to pay attention to the way Ash was looking at her body. If she did, they'd end up right back in bed again and probably starve to death. "What were you planning on making? There's one egg, and I couldn't find any bread or bacon. I used what you had last weekend. Don't you ever shop for groceries? I mean, if you were planning on this happening when you made dinner for me last night, why in God's name didn't you pick up any other food?"

"I wasn't thinking past last night," Ash told her with a slight smile.

"We can go by the hotel so I can put on my own clothes. Not that wearing yours isn't enticing, and just a wee bit erotic, but my shoulders are a little broader than yours." Jordan dried off quickly and put Ash's T-shirt on to prove her point. She might as well have been wearing a child's shirt it was so tight in the chest and shoulders.

"Mmm," Ash said with a nod, her eyes fixed squarely on her chest. "Your breasts are slightly larger than mine too."

"Slightly?" Jordan shook her head and smiled at her in the mirror. When their eyes met, Jordan had to grab the counter before her legs gave out. "Don't look at me like that."

"You didn't seem to mind it last night. Or this morning, for that matter."

"We weren't trying to do anything standing up then." Jordan turned to face her and tried to keep her hands from shaking. She wasn't entirely sure if it was from wanting to touch Ash, or the MS. Or lack of food. Maybe it was all three.

She took a step toward her. "And for the record, I want you to look at me that way when we're in bed."

"So noted."

"Spoken like a true cop." Jordan escorted her out of the room and closed the door so she could get dressed in peace. She couldn't think when Ash was around, and that wasn't good. She needed to make sure Ash knew where they stood before things got truly out of hand, if they hadn't already.

When Ash wasn't standing in front of her, or flat on her back underneath her, everything was so clear in Jordan's mind. But when they were together, Jordan had trouble remembering why she needed to keep things casual between them. But things were already beyond casual. How could it not be with Ash? She should have known better than to give in, but she *was* in, and she had no desire to get out.

"You are so screwed, Stryker," she said to her reflection. "You need to grow a pair and learn to say no to her."

But it was so easy to say yes. To just close her eyes and forget anything existed outside of the moment and the two of them. Because when she was with Ash, that was all that mattered. Just them. The thought of leaving Vegas and never seeing her again threatened to make her physically ill.

"Then don't think about it," she said. "At least not until you have to start your tournament tomorrow. Just enjoy it for what it is and deal with the aftermath later."

God, if it were only that simple.

CHAPTER TWENTY-FOUR

Ash leaned back in her chair when the waitress brought their plates to the table. She'd been craving the waffles she was looking at, but when she saw Jordan's eggs Benedict set in front of her, she considered whether or not she'd be able to distract Jordan long enough to switch their plates. Knowing she'd never get away with it, she spread the butter liberally over her waffles before drowning them in syrup.

"Are you sure you don't want some waffles with all that syrup?" Jordan teased her when they were alone again.

"Shut up and eat your damn breakfast."

"Ooh, testy. You covet my food, don't you?"

"Fuck you," Ash said, trying to be serious but failing miserably.

"Later you can fuck me all you want." Jordan spoke quietly as she leaned as far across the table as she could. Ash squirmed in her seat at the sexy tone of her voice and the arousal that swept through her body with the visual Jordan's words elicited. When Jordan sat back she cut a piece of egg and English muffin and held the fork out to Ash. "But for now, have a bite."

Ash didn't wait to be asked twice. She leaned in, closed her lips around the food, and pulled it off the fork, all while holding Jordan's gaze. She was amazed as she watched Jordan's eyes grow incredibly dark.

"Hello, ladies."

Ash looked up and saw Jan standing next to their table. She glanced at Jordan and was surprised to see recognition in her features.

"Jan," Ash said with a nod. "What are you doing here?"

"I was walking by in the casino and saw you two sitting here," she answered. "I thought I'd come and say hello. How are you, Jordan?"

"Very well, thank you."

"I heard you won the no-limit hold 'em tourney, congratulations."

"How do you know each other?" Ash tried hard to not show her jealous side, but Jordan's smirk told her she wasn't succeeding.

"Well, we met at the bar last Saturday night, although Jordan doesn't remember much about it from what I understand," Jan said, her smile a little too feral for Ash's liking. "And I ran into her last Sunday night outside Starbucks."

"I was there hoping you might be there," Jordan told Ash. She reached across the table and covered Ash's hand with her own.

Ash smiled when she saw the maneuver had the desired effect. Jan looked at their joined hands before looking at each of them and nodding, her expression unreadable. She left without another word, and Ash let out the laugh she was holding in as soon as she was far enough away she couldn't hear.

"She wants you in the worst way," Ash said, pulling her hand away and going back to her waffles.

"I don't want her." Jordan stared at her until Ash finally met her eyes. "I don't want anyone but you. She did try to pick me up, but I told her I wasn't interested."

"Jan's a friend, but the woman tries to pick up anything that has a vagina."

"Oh, ouch," Jordan said with a wince.

"I'm sorry. Did I bruise your ego?"

"Bruise? I think you may have crushed it for good."

"You do know you're not just *anything that has a vagina*, right? You are so out of her league on so many different levels."

"Nice save, Ms. Noble." Jordan's eyes flashed with what Ash could only call desire. "Hurry and eat your breakfast so we can grab a few things from my room and get back to your place. If we're fast enough, the bed might still be warm."

❖

They never did make it back to Ash's house, instead finding the hotel room bed to be quite satisfactory. Jordan was on her back, Ash's body draped across hers, and Ash's head on her chest. Ash was asleep, but Jordan couldn't clear her mind enough to allow sleep to claim her.

Jordan closed her eyes, trying not to let Ash's exhales mere millimeters from her nipple affect her. It was a losing battle. Ash stirred slightly, an arm going around Jordan's waist and holding onto her tightly.

She was elated to have Ash back in her life, back in her bed. She was the only woman Jordan had ever loved, but that wasn't something she'd ever told anyone. She allowed her hand to move in slow circles on Ash's back as she stared at the ceiling.

She tried to put herself in Ash's place. Would she want to get involved with someone who had a disease like MS? An illness that could potentially rob her of her functionality, of her ability to communicate? The answer surprised her.

If it was Ash, it wouldn't matter.

But how could that be? Why would anyone want to enter into a relationship with someone who might only have a handful of years left to be self-sufficient? Even if she were willing to do it if Ash was the one who had MS, it wasn't something she could ask of her. Ash deserved a partner who was whole, and who would be whole for many years to come. She sighed and tried to untangle herself from Ash's arms and legs.

"Don't you dare think about leaving this bed," Ash said against her skin. "You're so warm."

"I need to go to the bathroom. Surely you wouldn't deny me that, would you? I don't think the maid would be very happy if I wet the bed." Jordan kissed her forehead before Ash finally rolled off her and settled in to apparently go back to sleep. "I'll be right back."

"Promise?"

"I promise."

Jordan went into the bathroom and did what she needed to do. After she washed her hands she set about getting her medication ready to inject. Just as she was about to inject it into her upper arm, Ash tried to come in, but Jordan had locked the door. Ash knocked.

"Jordan, I need to come in."

"Give me just a minute," she called back. She could hear Ash grumbling on the other side of the door.

She quickly did the injection and hurried to put everything away. She gave the counter one more look to make sure she hadn't missed anything before unlocking the door. Ash pushed past her and ran to the toilet.

"What took you so long?" Ash asked.

"I didn't know I did." Jordan left the room before Ash had an opportunity to press the issue. She pulled on a pair of shorts and a shirt just as Ash came back out looking disappointed.

"You're dressed," she said, an adorable pout on her lips. Jordan pulled her close and kissed her but pulled away before it had an opportunity to become passionate.

"I am. And you should get dressed too. I want to take you to dinner."

"Where?" Ash seemed pleased by the prospect.

"Anywhere your heart desires."

"Then can we go back to my place? I didn't check to make sure Trixie had food and water before we left this morning."

"Absolutely," Jordan said. "Wouldn't want the little fuzzball to start hating me."

Jordan sat on the foot of the bed and watched Ash as she got dressed. She needed to do something. It was getting too easy to fall into a routine with Ash. It was time to tell her she'd be going home soon. She really wasn't looking forward to *that* conversation. She smiled when Ash stepped into her shorts wrong and almost fell over. Jordan reached out to steady her, and Ash ended up in her lap.

Hell, they could always talk tomorrow, right?

CHAPTER TWENTY-FIVE

Jordan didn't do nearly as well in her second tournament as she'd done in the first. She was eliminated halfway through the second day. It didn't bother her nearly as much as she thought it would, and she gave credit to Ash for that. Or maybe it had something to do with the six-figure check, her winnings from the first tourney, sitting in the safe in the lobby. Either way, she was okay with losing, as long as it didn't translate into a loss during the Main Event.

It was the Fourth of July, and Jordan was waiting in Starbucks for Ash's shift to end. She'd worked the morning shift so they could make it to Mark's grandmother's house for her picnic and to watch the fireworks. Jordan was surprised at how easily she was fitting in to things in Vegas, and in Ash's life. She still hadn't had the dreaded conversation with Ash, and the more time that went by, and the more comfortable she felt, the harder it was for her to separate herself from everything going on around her. This felt right to her on so many levels, but she knew she had to put the brakes on. Soon. Just not on the Fourth of July.

But if not today, when? The big tournament, the Main Event, started the next morning, and although she didn't start playing until Monday, Ash was going to be working longer shifts because of the influx of people in the casino. She took a drink of her coffee and decided she would just have to make the time to have the conversation. It wasn't like they were spending a whole lot of time sleeping.

"Hey, you," Ash said into her ear.

She tried not to show how the low, sultry voice affected her, but the goose bumps on her arms gave her away. She smiled and turned in her seat to look at Ash.

"Hey, yourself. I was just waiting for my date to show up, but maybe I'd rather spend the rest of my day with you. If we hurry, we might make it out of here before she shows up." She lifted her eyebrows suggestively and Ash laughed. That beautifully wonderful laugh that made Jordan feel all warm and gooey inside.

"You really want to risk her being angry with you?" Ash asked as she took a seat. Jordan glanced under the table at the long, toned legs Ash's shorts revealed. Definitely not work attire, so obviously she'd changed in her office.

"Wrap those incredible legs around me and I won't care how angry she gets."

"Fuck, Jordan," Ash said under her breath as she looked around.

"Yes, exactly." Jordan glanced around too, but there was nobody close enough to hear their conversation. She smiled as Ash crossed her legs and looked rather uncomfortable at being in public.

"Do you have any idea how hard it's going to be to get through the rest of the day?"

"Mmm." Jordan nodded. "Hard being the key word."

"Jesus." Ash stood abruptly and towered over her. "Let's go now so maybe we can leave early."

"Early? It's the Fourth of July." Jordan stood too and they walked out of Starbucks side by side. "There's no such thing as leaving early on the Fourth or New Year's Eve, because the whole point of the festivities is they take place at night."

❖

"Jordan, this is Kelly Osgood," Ash said when he came to greet them, beers in hand. She took one and tipped the bottle in thanks before taking a drink. "We call him Oz, but don't make any wizard jokes, because he's really sensitive."

"So noted." Jordan held a hand out and he shook it with a nod.

"It's a pleasure to finally meet you, Jordan," he said.

Jordan looked at Ash, an obvious question in her eyes. Ash didn't really want to admit she'd talked about Jordan with Oz, or anyone else for that matter, but it looked like she was going to have to now. Perhaps she should have said something to him beforehand.

"Finally?" Jordan asked.

"I've heard so much about you over the years, it's just nice to be able to put a face with the name."

"Really. Interesting." Jordan put an arm around Ash's waist and pulled her close, her lips just inches from Ash's ear. "So you've talked about me a lot, have you?"

Ash nodded and tried not to let on that the warm breath in her ear was turning her on. She turned her head and gave Jordan a quick kiss on the lips.

"He works with me, but he's also a friend. We talk." Ash shrugged, hoping Jordan would let it go. Oz was the only one she'd told that she'd been in love with Jordan when they had their affair.

"I brought a date," Oz said as he looked around. "I don't want to leave her alone for too long or else somebody else might try to pick her up. I'll catch up with you guys later though, all right?"

"Sure," Ash said.

"Nice to meet you, Oz," said Jordan. They stood there in silence for a few minutes, Jordan looking like she was uncomfortable being around so many people she didn't know.

"Come on," Ash said, taking Jordan's hand and leading her toward the house. "I'll introduce you to Mark's grandmother."

She said hello to a few people on the way, and introduced Jordan to some of them. When they finally made their way onto the back porch, Ash opened the screen door and walked in. She'd been there so many times in the six years she'd been in Vegas she was beginning to feel like family. She had to admit it was nice to feel like she *had* a family again.

"Sherry?" she called as they stood in the empty kitchen.

"I'm in the living room," came the reply. "Damn desert heat's going to be the death of me. I can't stay outside for very long at all anymore. Thank God for central air conditioning."

"Don't think you can survive the Vegas summers without it," Ash said. Sherry stood from where she'd been seated on the couch and Ash allowed herself to be enveloped in a hug. Sherry was a large woman, close to Ash's height, but she weighed a good fifty pounds more. When they stepped back from their hug, Sherry eyed Jordan.

"And who is this?" she asked.

"This is Jordan Stryker. Jordan, this is Mark's grandmother, Sherry."

"That's not possible," Jordan said, looking truly perplexed. "Mark would have to be ten for that to be mathematically possible."

"Oh, she's good," Sherry said with a laugh and a wink for Ash. She pulled Jordan into a hug and planted a kiss on her cheek. When she backed away, she placed a hand on Jordan's cheek. "And one hell of a looker, too. But if you ever hurt Ashley, your good looks won't keep you out of trouble with me, understand?"

"Perfectly," Jordan answered, looking a little frightened of what this woman might do to her.

Ash watched the exchange with interest. She realized long ago that the people she'd met since moving to Vegas were the only family she needed. Sherry was a mother figure even though she was only fourteen years older than Ash. Sherry had only been thirty-two when her grandson was born.

"Do you know Mark?" Sherry asked Jordan.

"Yes, I do."

"Good. Follow me." Sherry led them back into the kitchen where she took a plate of hamburgers and chicken breasts out of the refrigerator. She shoved the plate into Jordan's hands. "Take this to him and tell him it's time to start cooking."

Jordan nodded and glanced at Ash before hurrying out the back door. Sherry motioned for Ash to follow her back to the living room where they sat side by side on the couch.

"I think you've put the fear of God in her, Sherry," Ash said, not able to keep from laughing.

"Good. Not enough young people fear God nowadays."

Ash nodded her agreement, but didn't point out Jordan was only eleven years younger than Sherry. And she wasn't even sure Jordan believed in God anyway, but it didn't really matter because Sherry had accomplished what she'd set out to do—letting Jordan know she'd have to answer to someone if she hurt Ash.

"You've never brought a date to my house before. Is this one special?"

"Yeah, she is," Ash answered.

"Where did you meet her?" Sherry smiled and patted Ash's leg. "Tell me everything."

Ash did, minus the speculation about the MS. Sherry already knew some of the circumstances surrounding her departure from Los Angeles, but Ash had never told her about the affair with Jordan. When she finished her story, she held her breath as she waited for Sherry's response. Sherry shook her head for a moment before finally looking at her.

"Is this thing between you going to last this time?"

"I hope so, but I know I broke her heart before by not being honest with her." Ash held her head in her hands. "But now she's not being honest with me. I know there's more to the reason she left the FBI, but she just keeps saying she got burned out and decided to pursue other things."

"Maybe there isn't anything more to it, sweetie," Sherry said. "But at any rate, her reasons brought her here and back to you."

"You sound like Maria." Ash chuckled. "Everything happens for a reason, right?"

"Maria's a smart cookie. How is she doing?"

"She's doing well. She's in the wheelchair, but for the most part she does everything for herself."

"Tell her I said hi and we missed her and her husband here this year." Sherry got to her feet and held a hand out to Ash. "Maybe we should head out back and see what mischief Mark and his friends have gotten Jordan into."

CHAPTER TWENTY-SIX

Jordan stood near Mark and watched as his friends tried to get a game of football going. There were probably about thirty people there for the picnic, which was an impressive turnout as far as Jordan was concerned. She'd never attended a picnic with more than about ten people.

"Come on, Jordan, you look like you'd make a good wide receiver," one of the guys hollered to her. He was the quarterback of one of the teams, and she was pretty sure Mark had introduced him as Jeff.

"Hey, I don't know why you have to use that cane of yours sometimes, but don't let them bully you into playing," Mark said. "Besides, I think if you got hurt, Ash would have my head."

"Yeah, you're probably right about that." Jordan smiled to herself. It was rather nice to have a protector. She shook her head and held her hand up. "Not today, guys, sorry."

"They're only out there trying to show off anyway," Mark said. She watched him flip the burgers like he'd been doing it his whole life. "For some reason they think they have to prove their masculinity."

"But not you?"

"Hell no. I played football in high school. I'm done proving anything to anybody. And I'm quite happy with who I am, thank you very much."

"Good for you," Jordan said as she held her beer bottle up to salute him.

"There you are," Ash said as she and Sherry walked up to them. Jordan leaned into her when Ash put an arm around her shoulders. "I was worried they'd talk you into playing."

"Oh, believe me, they tried," Mark said. "But girlfriend here is secure in her masculinity. Or her femininity, whichever she chooses to display."

"Here's to being comfortable in your own skin," Jordan said. Mark picked up his beer and they all tapped their bottles together before taking a drink.

"Hey, Ash," Jeff said as he ran over to them. "We need another player. Please?"

"Sorry, fellas, I'm just watching this year." Ash smiled when Jeff pouted and walked back to the game looking dejected.

"You can play if you want," Jordan told her. She didn't want Ash feeling like she needed to babysit her.

"I'd rather just be on the sidelines with you." Ash gave her a quick kiss on the lips.

"Now wait a minute, I thought you two were *just friends*." Mark stood with one hand on his hip and the other waving the spatula he was using to flip the burgers.

"We've never been *just friends*," Ash replied with a grin.

"We tried it for a few days, but it didn't work for us," Jordan said in agreement.

"Lesbians," he muttered under his breath as he shook his head.

"Mind your manners," Sherry told him with a swat to his shoulder. He feigned being hurt and she just laughed at him. "Like gay men are any better."

"At least we don't bring a U-Haul to the second date, Granny." He smiled and stuck his tongue out at them, which earned him a harder sounding swat.

"That joke's a little old, isn't it?" Jordan asked.

"Ignore him and he'll stop," Ash told her. She held up her beer bottle. "You want another?"

"No, I think I'll stick to soda for the rest of the day." Jordan watched as Ash went to find them new drinks. She wasn't really against alcohol, but she had cut down quite a bit when her mother was diagnosed with dementia. But since she'd been in Vegas, she felt like she had a drink in her hand every time she turned around. And she loved the fact Ash didn't question her decision to not drink.

There was a lot she was finding to love about Ash, and about being in Las Vegas, and it scared her. She was becoming too comfortable. It was just so damn easy though. The people were so laid-back and welcoming, and what was waiting for her back in Philadelphia anyway? She didn't honestly know why she'd even decided to stay there when she left the bureau. It wasn't as if she had many friends there. She was simply tired of moving and didn't want to face it again.

Matt was in Phoenix and had been bugging her to move back home ever since she quit. The time she'd spent at the field office in Portland had been some of the best times of her life. And now there was a reason to consider Las Vegas. But was it really an option?

Other than her three-day-a-week injection and the occasional day when she needed her cane, she'd been able to put her MS in the back of her mind. She wasn't so sure that was a smart move though. There had always been times when she'd hoped there'd been a misdiagnosis, that she didn't really have MS. But then she'd have the inevitable relapse and realize thinking that way was nothing more than a fantasy.

And really, wasn't that what she was doing here? Fantasizing about having a life she would never be able to have? She took a seat at a picnic table where she could watch them playing football. Before she realized there was something wrong with her, she'd have been right out there with them.

But fooling herself and Ash into believing they could have something lasting wasn't doing either of them any good. She'd be gone at the end of the tournament, which at the most, would be about seven more days, and that was only if she made it to the final table. She raked a hand through her hair and sighed loudly.

"You okay?" Ash asked as she set a can of Coke in front of her. She put a hand on Jordan's back as she sat next to her.

"Fine," she said with a smile and a quick nod of her head. "Just watching the game."

The look Ash gave her told Jordan she didn't fully believe her, but Jordan had no desire to bring up her leaving. Not today. There was always tomorrow.

The problem was, she was running out of tomorrows.

Ash sat on the ground with Jordan in a chair behind her, her head resting against Jordan's thigh. The fireworks would be starting any minute. She closed her eyes when Jordan's fingers began gently massaging her scalp.

"You two need anything?" she heard Sherry ask.

"No, we're good," Jordan told her. "Sit down and relax. Enjoy the fireworks."

"I intend to do just that," Sherry said before walking away.

Ash had tried not to think about Jordan's impending departure, and she'd actually been successful for most of the time they'd been together over the past days. But today, when she'd brought her that can of Coke, Ash knew Jordan had been thinking about it. She could tell by the sad look on her face when she'd told Ash she was fine. And the rest of the day she'd been rather reserved and quiet, which wasn't really like her.

She'd hoped she could convince Jordan through her actions that things might actually work out for them, that a future together was possible, but unless Jordan was ready to tell her about her MS, she knew that future would never happen.

The Main Event was starting tomorrow, with Jordan's first day of action on Monday, which meant in nine more days the World Series of Poker would be done. At least the portion played now. The final round, which meant the nine players at the final table, wouldn't be played until mid-November. Jordan hadn't told her she was leaving, but she had given no indication she might stay when it was done either.

Of course, if Jordan made it to the final table, she'd have to come back again in four months. Ash didn't want to wait that long to see her again. She'd lost Jordan once due to her own reluctance. She had no intention of losing her again simply because Jordan was afraid of what the future held for her.

The first loud boom of the fireworks caused her to jump, and she felt Jordan's arms slide around her shoulders, pulling her back against her. This felt too good—too *right*—to only be a short affair. Ash covered Jordan's hands with her own to keep them where they were on her chest above her breasts.

She wasn't going to let her go without a fight.

CHAPTER TWENTY-SEVEN

Jordan was eliminated from the Main Event on day eight, her sixth day of play. If she'd managed to hold on for just one more day, she would have had a real shot at making it to the final table. She thought for sure she'd win that last hand with pocket kings, but no king came up in the flop, the turn, or the river. She'd lost to a guy who went all in with pocket deuces. She had the hand won until the river, when the dealer turned up another two.

She spent the rest of the day in her room, waiting for Ash's shift to end. She'd had five hours to sit and think about the bad beat, and it still pissed her off to realize she'd lost to an idiot who went all in on pocket deuces. But poker was ultimately a game of chance, and more often than not, luck trumped skill. She knew she'd done the right thing calling the bet, but that didn't make the loss any easier to take.

When it was almost time for Ash to punch out, she headed down to Starbucks to wait for her. It had become their routine during the past week, and it was beginning to become a little too comfortable. But she had to admit it was nice. But the time had come for her to head back to Philly. Unfortunately, she had no clue how to bring it up to Ash. It had been so easy to immerse herself in the fantasy they'd created, Jordan simply hadn't given much thought to it.

"I'm so sorry you lost, baby," Ash said as they walked into her house. She got a beer for each of them and they settled in on the couch. Trixie jumped up into Jordan's lap, which had become routine for her on the nights they stayed here.

"I came closer than I probably should have." Jordan shrugged it off and tried to fight the nervousness she was feeling. She concentrated on scratching Trixie's chin and chuckled when the cat stretched out on her lap.

"She really likes you."

"I never really liked cats, but she's kind of grown on me," Jordan admitted. Ash scooted closer on the couch and took Jordan's hand, lacing their fingers together. Jordan risked a look at Ash's face and saw the dismay there. It was obvious she was worried about what was going to happen to them now.

"You're going to leave, aren't you?" Ash was trying not to cry, and it chipped away at Jordan's resolve when she saw her eyes water. "Don't answer that right now. I just want to enjoy tonight. After tomorrow I'm off for a couple of days. Will you promise me you'll wait until then, so we can sit down and talk about it?"

"Ash…" Jordan swallowed hard and brushed the tears from Ash's cheeks with the backs of her fingers when they began to fall.

"I just want you to promise me you'll wait. I really don't want to get off work tomorrow night and find out you've disappeared," she explained.

Jordan nodded, but she could see Ash wasn't convinced. She wiped away another tear before leaning in and pressing her lips to Ash's. She looked her in the eyes and nodded again.

"I promise. I will not disappear tomorrow. I will wait until your days off so we can talk."

"Thank you," Ash said, her entire body sagging with relief. Jordan held her like that until they both fell asleep.

❖

They agreed Jordan would pack up her things and check out of the hotel so she could stay with Ash for a few days until she headed back to Philly. Jordan was surprised Ash hadn't asked her to do it earlier. It wasn't like they didn't spend every night together, either at Ash's house or Jordan's hotel room, but it was nice knowing if she'd wanted to, Jordan had a place to go to be by herself.

They got back to the house just in time for Ash to turn right around and go back to the hotel for the start of her shift. Jordan leaned against the counter in the kitchen with Trixie sitting on a chair at the table. They were engaged in an old-fashioned stare down. Jordan wondered briefly if the cat would turn on her now that they were alone for the first time. But after a few moments, the cat blinked lazily and she looked away before jumping down and trotting up the stairs.

She was looking for something to eat in Ash's barren cupboards and refrigerator when she realized they probably should have made a stop at the grocery store. How could anyone live like this? She found a pad of paper and a pen and started writing out a list before she realized she didn't really live there. It felt like she did, and the realization both scared and excited her. She shook her head and ripped the sheet of paper off the pad, balling it up in her fist and tossing it in the trash.

A can of soup, a loaf of bread, and perhaps something for breakfast would suffice until they could get to the store the next day. And maybe a bag of Doritos. She was suddenly craving Spicy Nacho Doritos. She grabbed the key Ash had left for her and ventured out to the store.

After putting things away, she took the bag of Doritos and a beer into the living room with her where she made herself comfortable on the couch. Only seven more hours, give or take a few minutes, before Ash would return home. She took a pull from the bottle and leaned her head back as she closed her eyes.

These past couple of weeks had been invigorating. More than once Jordan had found herself wondering if they could possibly make things work between them. But then she'd remember her disease was real, and it would eventually relapse. She couldn't just pretend everything was fine.

She knew the only person who could ever make her happy was Ash. But Ash deserved to have a future with someone who would be active for years to come. Not to be tied down to a lover as a caretaker. It wouldn't be fair to either of them.

Jordan had a feeling Ash would fight her every step of the way on this, which was why she had no intention of telling her about the MS. She still wasn't sure yet exactly what she was going to offer as reasoning behind her leaving, but it wouldn't be that.

She jumped with surprise when Trixie hopped in her lap, purring and rubbing her face against her hand. She flopped down and turned onto her back, showing Jordan she wanted her belly rubbed. Jordan smiled and did as the cat requested. The normalcy of the situation tried to take hold somewhere in her mind, but she refused to let it. She couldn't allow herself to think of being in Ash's house as normal. She would never have a *normal life*—at least not like other people did.

When her phone rang, she jerked, causing Trixie to take off running from where she'd been sleeping on Jordan's chest.

She saw by the clock on the wall it was a little after eight. She grabbed her phone, surprised to see her brother's name on the display.

"Matty, what's up?"

"I woke you up."

"No, I was just napping. Barely asleep." She sat up and stretched her back before running her hand through her hair. "Is everything all right?"

"No," he said, sounding so much like the little boy he used to be. He almost sounded as though he might cry at any moment. "Mom had a stroke."

"Shit, Matt. When?"

"This afternoon. They don't think she's going to make it. Something about an aneurysm. They want to do brain surgery but I told them they couldn't before you get here."

"What?" Jordan stood and paced in front of the couch. If she left in the morning, she could be there in the early afternoon. "Matt, they can't wait. Aneurysms are bad news. It could rupture and kill her almost instantly. Let them do the surgery, and I'll be there as soon as I can."

"She asked for you, Jordan."

She stopped pacing abruptly, not sure she heard him right. She shook her head but didn't say anything. It was strange enough to hear she even remembered having children, but to ask for Jordan of all people? She wiped away a tear and tried to swallow around the lump in her throat.

"You must have misunderstood what she said."

"No, Sis, she said, 'Where's Jordan? I want her here.' What's to misunderstand about that?"

"It'll take me almost four hours to get there, and I can't leave till morning."

"Why? If you left now, you could be here by midnight. Of course, the way you drive, maybe eleven."

"Very funny, smartass," she muttered. She couldn't leave. She promised Ash she wouldn't. If Ash came home and found her gone, Jordan knew she'd think she got scared and ran off. Even if she left a note, Jordan was pretty sure she'd still think it. But what choice did she have? Her mother asked for her. And Jordan knew damn well Matt would be a basket case if she didn't make it through surgery. She needed to be there for him if nothing else. "All right, I can probably get out of here by nine. I'll do my best to get there around midnight. Where should I go?"

They made arrangements to meet at the hospital, and Jordan made him promise her he wouldn't make the doctors wait if they decided she needed the surgery sooner rather than later. She hung up and immediately called Ash's cell phone but there was no answer and the recording claimed her voicemail was full. She decided to try the hotel, hoping they could transfer her to security. Speaking to her over the phone would be better than a note, right? They put her on hold and she ran upstairs to grab her things. By the time she was ready to walk out the door, she was finally transferred.

"Security, Jan speaking."

"Jan, it's Jordan. I need to speak with Ash right away."

"Sorry, Jordan, but she's in the middle of throwing out a belligerent drunk. She's probably outside with him waiting for the cops to get here. Can I take a message?"

Jordan thought about it for a moment and ultimately decided it would be the best way.

"My mother's had a stroke and I need to get back to Flagstaff ASAP. The doctors don't think she's going to make it, and my brother needs me there with him. Tell her I'm sorry, but I have to go."

"Sure, I can let her know."

"Thanks, Jan, I appreciate it."

Jordan hung up and was about to leave when she had a strange feeling Jan might not give Ash the message. It was a terrible thing to think about someone she barely knew, but Jan struck her as a bit of a flake. She got the pad and pen she'd used earlier to make the shopping list and quickly wrote out a note. It was probably better this way for both of them. Ash was going to hate her for saying good-bye this way, but just knowing she wasn't going to have to look at Ash when she told her good-bye made her anxiety levels drop.

Besides, she knew she'd never be able to say good-bye to her face-to-face, because all she could think about when Ash was around was how nice it would be to stay in Vegas and be with her. She wouldn't be able to walk away, but she knew she had to.

So yes, while it was easier this way, it certainly didn't make it hurt any less.

Chapter Twenty-eight

Ash felt her stomach sink when she pulled into the driveway and there weren't any lights on. Jordan had been parking her car in the garage so she reached up to where the opener was on the visor and took a deep breath before pushing the button. When she saw the garage was empty, she felt as though her heart might break into a thousand pieces. Jordan had promised she'd stay. Ash wasn't surprised though. It was obvious Jordan didn't want to tell her about her MS.

It pissed Ash off that Jordan felt she could arbitrarily make decisions that affected more than just herself. Didn't Ash have a say in what she wanted? She wanted Jordan, but Jordan was apparently taking herself out of the equation for her. Why hadn't she found out where in Philadelphia Jordan lived? She fumed in her car for a few minutes before finally getting out and slamming the door in frustration.

Once inside she noticed a half-empty beer bottle on the coffee table and an unopened bag of Doritos next to it. Maybe she hadn't left, Ash thought, feeling hopeful for a moment. Maybe she just ran out to the store. Ash went upstairs and looked in the drawers she'd cleaned out for Jordan. They were empty. Her suitcase was gone. Everything was gone. She grabbed the phone and dialed Jordan's cell, but she must have had it turned off because it went right to voicemail. Ash collapsed onto the bed and promised herself she wouldn't cry.

She succeeded for all of five minutes, which was how long it took for Trixie to find her and curl up on her chest, purring as if nothing in the world had changed. She closed her eyes and willed herself not to think about Jordan. She was exhausted after having to work so many days in a row, and even though she couldn't keep Jordan out of her mind, she drifted off to sleep in just a few minutes.

❖

Jordan arrived at the hospital at the same time she knew Ash would be getting home from work. She tried not to think about it as she rushed to the entrance and asked the woman at the desk for her brother. A few minutes went by before Matt came walking down the corridor to her right. Jordan almost lost it when she saw he'd been crying.

"Is she…" Jordan couldn't finish the question. The lump in her throat was too big. She pulled him into a fierce hug. She'd never been close with her mother, but it still hurt to think she'd arrived too late.

"She's in surgery now. They took her in about forty-five minutes ago. They said they couldn't wait any longer."

"I'm so sorry I didn't get here in time to see her before surgery, Matty, but she's a fighter. She'll pull through this."

"I hope you're right. We should get back up to the waiting room. The doctor said someone would find me there to give me updates."

Jordan nodded and followed him to the elevators. They were the only people in the surgical waiting area, and Jordan was grateful. She really didn't want to deal with any people.

They took two comfortable but really ugly yellow chairs against the wall and sat in silence as they waited for an update. Jordan looked around the room, noticing it could have been any room in any hospital she'd ever been in with its drab gray walls and institutional flooring.

She pulled her phone out before remembering she'd turned it off when she left Ash's house. She decided to leave it off. She really wasn't in any state of mind to talk to Ash at the moment. She was surprised to realize she was hurting over the possible loss of her mother. When their father had died, she couldn't have cared less. She assumed it would be the same with her mother, but it wasn't. Maybe there really was some kind of special bond between a mother and child. Funny, she'd never felt it before.

New tears sprang forth when Matt reached over and clasped her hand. He'd never sought comfort before. Their father had drilled into him that men don't cry, and they certainly never allowed their emotions to show. She held on to him tightly and leaned over to lay her head on his shoulder. After a moment, he rested his head against hers, and Jordan fell asleep after a few minutes.

❖

When Ash awoke, the sun was just starting to rise. Her bedroom faced the east and she hadn't thought to close the curtains the night before so it was shining in her eyes. Trixie had moved so she was lying against her shoulder, snoring softly in her ear. She stared at the ceiling, wondering why she should even bother getting up. She didn't have to be at work for two days, and Jordan leaving without a word certainly seemed like a good excuse for a pity party.

She shook her head and sat up, wincing at the way her back protested. Sleeping on her back with her feet flat on the floor apparently didn't agree with her. She stood and stretched until she felt a satisfying pop in her spine. She glanced at the rumpled clothes she hadn't bothered taking off the night before. Coffee or shower?

Without giving too much thought to it, she stripped and walked into the bathroom. When she was done, Trixie was curled up in the clothes she'd left on the floor. She pulled on a pair of shorts and a T-shirt before heading down to make coffee. When she walked into the kitchen, her steps faltered at the sight of a piece of paper taped to the coffee maker. Her heart felt like someone squeezed it and she mentally berated herself for not looking in the kitchen last night.

She grabbed it and leaned against the counter to read.

Ash,

I'm so sorry to leave this way. I really did intend to stay as I promised. I got a call from my brother. My mother's had a stroke and I need to be there. If not for her, then for Matt. He still has this idyllic picture of her in his head, and if she dies, it might just send him over the edge.

I tried to call you at work, but your cell went directly to voicemail, and I finally got in touch with Jan. Hopefully, she gave you the message I left, but if not, I decided I'd leave you this note just in case.

Maybe it's better this way, Ash. I can't stay in Vegas with you. I told you it was complicated, but I'm not sure how I could even begin to explain it to you. Please know that I love you. I will always love you, but we just can't be together.

Love,
Jordan

Ash stared at the words, the tears in her eyes making it difficult to read. But she didn't need to read the part where Jordan said she left a message with Jan again. A message she never received. Still gripping the note in her hand, Ash grabbed the phone and dialed Jan.

"'Lo?" Jan asked after the third ring.

"Did I wake you? Sorry." She paced as she tried to control her breathing. She definitely was not sorry for waking her, and she was sure her tone conveyed that. "Is there maybe something you want to tell me?"

"Ash? Is that you?" There was muffled noise in the background. Ash didn't know if she was disentangling herself from another body or if she was just trying to look at the clock, and she didn't care. "Jesus, what time is it?"

"Seven."

"In the morning? Fuck. What's wrong?"

"Do you have something to tell me?"

"I don't know what you're talking about."

"Did Jordan call and leave a message for me last night?"

The intake of breath and silence that followed answered her question. Ash slammed the note down on the counter and pinched the bridge of her nose between her thumb and forefinger.

"Where was I when she called, and why the fuck didn't you give me the message?"

"You were waiting for the cops with that asshole drunk, and I completely forgot about the message by the time you got back to the office. Jesus, I'm sorry, Ash."

"What was the message? Did she say where she was going?"

"Her mother had a stroke, I think. She said she was going to…fuck, I can't remember."

"Think about it." Ash was trying hard to be patient. She was sure Jan hadn't deliberately forgotten to give her the message. She could be a bit of an airhead at times. It had probably been an honest mistake. That didn't make it any easier to deal with now though. "I think she said she'd been in Arizona to visit her mother in a nursing home before she came to Vegas if that helps to jog your memory."

"Flagstaff!" Jan said after a moment. "She was in a hospital in Flagstaff."

"Thanks."

"Hey, Ash, I really am sorry."

Ash didn't say anything as she disconnected the call. She went upstairs to the room she used as a home office and powered up her laptop. There couldn't be that many hospitals in Flagstaff, could there?

Ten minutes later, she had the address for the Flagstaff Medical Center and a plan. It wasn't necessarily a good plan, but she wasn't about to let Jordan get away without a fight. She let her go once. She wasn't going to make the same mistake again.

CHAPTER TWENTY-NINE

Jordan opened her eyes and saw a man in scrubs walking toward them. She nudged Matt hard with her elbow. He quickly sat up straight and rubbed his eyes. Jordan wasn't sure she wanted to hear what this man had to say. She wasn't ready to say good-bye to her mother yet.

"Mr. Stryker, I just wanted to let you know your mother is resting comfortably." The man's name was Gary Mills, according to the ID badge he wore on the left side of his chest.

"Thank you, Dr. Mills," Matt said, sounding relieved.

"When can we see her?" Jordan asked.

"I'm sorry, who are you?"

"This is my sister, Jordan."

"Your mother was asking for you just before we put her under for the surgery." He smiled before running a hand over his bald head. "I'm sure she'll be happy you're here."

"When can we see her?" Jordan asked again. She wasn't convinced her mother *would* be happy she was there, so she chose not to respond to his remark.

"She's in recovery now. We'll need to keep an eye on her for a while, but I'm hoping to get her moved to a private room this afternoon. You can see her then. In the meantime, I suggest you both go get something to eat and perhaps go back to your hotel for some rest in a real bed. I'm certain these chairs aren't very comfortable to sleep in. Someone will come to let you know when you can see her. If you aren't here, we'll call the cell number you provided, Mr. Stryker."

"Thank you, again," Matt said, grasping the doctor's hand briefly.

"Is she going to be all right?" Jordan asked, putting voice to the question she knew Matt was afraid to ask.

"I honestly can't say what kind of permanent damage there may be from the stroke she suffered. Something you need to be aware of though, she doesn't have control of the facial muscles on the right side. And as with any brain surgery, there's always a chance of complications. She isn't out of the woods yet, but I'm cautiously optimistic about her chances."

When the doctor left them, Jordan glanced at the clock on the far wall. She couldn't believe it was ten thirty in the morning. Twelve hours earlier, she was halfway between Vegas and Flagstaff.

"Why don't we go grab something to eat?" she suggested.

"Yeah, I think there's a cafeteria somewhere."

"No, not hospital food." Jordan shook her head. She hated the look of panic in his eyes. "The doctor said it would be a while. Let's get some real food. He has your cell number, right?"

Jordan felt more energized after they had breakfast, but there was still a hollow feeling in her stomach, and she was certain the ache in her heart would never go away. How could she have left Ash—twice?

"How did you do in your tournaments?" Matt asked as he looked at his phone for what felt to Jordan like the millionth time since they sat down.

"I won the first one, didn't do so well in the others."

"Hey, that's great you won one of them." He smiled, but Jordan knew he was distracted. He'd probably forget everything they talked about by the time they got back to the hospital. "What about the Main Event?"

"I entered, and I got knocked out on day six." Jordan still cringed inwardly when she thought about the pocket deuces that beat her.

"So what did you do when you weren't playing poker? I mean you were there for like three weeks, right?"

"Yeah." She debated whether to tell him about Ash. Part of her wanted to keep the past couple of weeks her own little secret, but another part wanted someone to tell her what she did was right. She could always count on Matty to back her up. "You remember when we were here for Mom's birthday before I went to Vegas?"

"Yeah," he answered, looking as though he were trying to remember what they'd talked about.

"I told you about a woman I had an affair with a long time ago. A woman who was married."

"Yeah, her name was Ashley, right? You said you fell in love with her."

Jordan nodded and looked down at her empty plate. She closed her eyes for a moment in an attempt to ward off the pain, but it didn't work. She swallowed around the lump in her throat and raised her eyes to look at him again.

"Believe it or not, she's now head of security at the hotel I was staying at, which is also the hotel the tournament was being played at."

"Wow, I bet that was awkward."

"It was, at first. But we spent some time together. She's divorced now, and she's a lesbian. She left her husband and LA six years ago."

"So, are you guys an item?"

"What? No. I told you I won't get involved with anyone because of the MS. I refuse to have anyone stay with me because they feel obligated." They were both silent, and she saw Matt looking at her the way he always did when he thought she was being dense. She held her hands out in front of her, palms up. "What?"

"Did you even tell her? Did you give her an opportunity to make a decision on her own? Does she want something with you? Do you with her?"

"No, I didn't tell her. What's the point? And do you always ask that many questions at once?"

"I do," he said with a nod. "I'm an FBI agent. You realize you only answered one of my questions though, right?"

"Technically two, because the answer addressed both of the first two questions." Jordan smiled at their bantering. It felt good. "And the answers to the last two? Yes, and yes."

"Then why the hell are you here alone? Knowing you, you probably left without even telling her, didn't you?"

"I left her a note."

"Jesus, Jordan."

"Look, you're supposed to be on my side."

"I am on your side. I will always be on your side. But you're being stubborn. If she makes you happy, why not give it a chance?"

"Because Ashley Noble deserves better than to be stuck caring for someone with MS."

❖

Ash parked her vehicle and ran to the front doors of the hospital. She tried to catch her breath before approaching the desk. She wasn't sure how Jordan was going to react to her just showing up out of the blue and she wanted to be as calm and collected as possible.

"May I help you?" the woman behind the desk asked with a friendly smile.

"I hope so. I believe you have a patient here with the last name Stryker. She would have come in last night after a stroke?"

Ash waited as the woman typed something into the computer. "Yes, we do have a woman with that name here. May I ask what your relationship is to her?"

"I'm not related. I need to speak to her daughter. Could you please page Jordan Stryker for me? It's an emergency."

The woman looked skeptical but after a moment got onto the PA system and paged Jordan. Ash took her first deep breath since leaving Vegas four hours earlier.

"You can wait over there in the lobby." She pointed to a group of chairs and dismissed her. "I'll send her over when she comes down."

"Thank you…" Ash looked at her nametag then back into her eyes. "Betty. You have no idea how important this is."

Ash went to the lobby but couldn't sit still. She paced as she waited. After a few moments, she saw a man walk to the desk. He looked so much like Jordan there was no doubt in her mind he had to be her brother. She watched as Betty pointed toward her and then the man was on his way over.

"Hello," he said warily as he held a hand out in greeting. "I'm Matthew Stryker, Jordan's brother. Can I help you?"

"I need to see Jordan. Is she here?"

"Who are you?"

"I'm sorry, how rude of me." She shook his hand and tried to smile, but all she could think about was how Jordan probably didn't want to see her. "My name is Ashley Noble, if that means anything to you—"

"It does, actually. Jordan was just talking about you at breakfast this morning." He motioned for her to follow him outside the front entrance. "She isn't here right now. I convinced her to go to my hotel room and rest for a bit. We were both up most of the night waiting for news about our mother."

"Wow, I'm sorry, again." She chided herself and tried to get her head where it was supposed to be. "How is your mother doing?"

"As well as can be expected. It's still going to be a few hours before they'll let us see her, which is why I sent Jordan away."

"I don't know what she told you, but I'm begging you to help me. I need to talk to her."

He looked away for a moment and shook his head, obviously waging a battle in his head as to whether he should help. He mumbled something under his breath she couldn't make out, and she thought maybe she should strengthen her position.

"Look, I know you don't know me, but I love her. I love your sister, and I hope to God she's not in the closet with you." She felt her face flush but she refused to look away when he turned toward her. She relaxed when he laughed.

"She's not, but I think she'd be pretty pissed at you if you outed her to me or anyone else. In fact, she's going to be pissed at me for this, but the hotel is down the street about a mile on the left. Room two twelve."

"Thank you," she said before giving him a quick kiss on the cheek. "I'll tell her I held you at gunpoint for the information."

She heard him laughing as she ran back to her car. She only hoped she and Jordan would be laughing together soon.

CHAPTER THIRTY

Jordan had taken a quick shower and was just about to crawl into the bed when there was a knock at the door. She smiled because she knew Matt would follow her back here. He had to be exhausted. She was just happy he'd gotten a room with two double beds.

"Hold your horses, Matty." She turned the deadbolt and pulled the door open to a sight that stopped her in her tracks. Ash stood before her looking nervous and mad as hell at the same time. "What are you doing here?"

"You promised we could talk, so I'm here to talk." Ash pushed her way past Jordan without an invitation. There was no doubt she was angry with Jordan, and she couldn't blame her. "You're going to explain to me what about your life is so damn complicated that you refuse to enter into a relationship when you've made it pretty clear you love me."

Jordan sighed and ran a hand through her hair as she took a seat at the small table in front of the only window in the room. This place was a far cry from the Rio All Suites Hotel and Casino, but it was nice enough for a short stay.

"How did you find me?"

"I came home last night and was pissed you'd left without a word." Ash waved her off when Jordan started to protest. "I didn't see your note until this morning. You were right, Jan didn't give me the message, but I called her right away and she told me you were in Flagstaff, which I assume is something you left out of the note on purpose. There's only one hospital in Flagstaff, so finding it was pretty easy once I made up my mind I was coming after you. I met your brother, by the way. Nice guy. I promised him I'd swear I held him at gunpoint until he told me where you were."

"Sure you did," Jordan said, unable to stop the smile forming on her lips. After a moment of contemplating what to tell Ash, she shrugged. "I'm sorry, but I did try to call you."

"The battery in my phone died as soon as I got to work yesterday. I tried to call you when I realized you were gone."

"I turned the phone off. I didn't want to talk to you."

"Too bad, because now it looks like you don't have a choice."

Jordan nodded. She certainly couldn't argue the point. She'd never realized Ash was such a feisty one. She begrudgingly admitted she liked the quality in her. If she'd reacted this way when Ash ended their affair, who knew where they might be now? But no, she thought as she shook her head slightly, we're here now, together, because of everything that's happened in the past fifteen years. Neither of them had been ready for a permanent commitment back then. Ash had thought she was, which was why she'd chosen to stay with her husband.

"I can't explain to you why I can't be in a relationship."

"Bullshit." Ash began to pace between the two beds. "You've already told me you're single, right?"

Jordan nodded mutely.

"And you're not dying?"

"No."

Ash continued to pace and Jordan watched the subtle shifts in her facial expressions as she apparently thought about what to ask next. She stopped a couple of times and looked at Jordan, but then she'd shake her head and start pacing again. Finally, she threw her hands in the air and sat on the edge of the bed less than a foot from Jordan. The intensity in Ash's eyes almost made her crumble. But she resolved Ash would never know about her MS.

"Fine, Stryker, if you won't talk about the elephant in the room, then allow me." Ash took a deep breath and blew it out. She only called her by her last name when she was pissed about something. "You have multiple sclerosis and you're scared to death about what the future holds for you. You don't want anyone feeling sorry for you, and I get that, I really do. But if you think I'd stay with you just because I felt sorry for you, then you don't know me very well."

Jordan sat there, stunned. Where had all that come from? From the box of medication on the bathroom counter in the hotel? She felt her mouth moving, trying to speak, but there was nothing coming out.

"I saw your meds," Ash told her as though she could read her mind. "I recognized it as the same thing Maria takes. I did some research into MS, and it doesn't have to be as scary as you or I think it might be."

"So you've known since the night you took me to the hotel from the bar?" Jordan was happy to rediscover her voice, but it sounded strange to her. Almost like she was about to cry. "How could you not have told me?"

"You mean like you told me about it instead of just saying *it's complicated*? Jesus, Jordan, I figured you didn't want to talk about it, so I didn't want to bring it up. I kept trying to get you to talk, but you can be so damned stubborn sometimes."

"I take it Maria knows?"

"Yes. I needed to talk to someone about it."

"The day we went to the Grand Canyon, you were inside the store paying for the gas, and she tried to get me to admit I had MS." Jordan looked at her, trying to discern if it had been Ash's plan all along to trick her into confessing it to Maria. As far as she could tell, Ash was as genuinely surprised by it as Jordan had been. "I wondered for a moment if you'd put her up to it, or if she just noticed little things most people wouldn't as being symptoms for MS."

"I didn't put her up to it, Jordan. And if I'd known she would do that, I never would have talked to her about it."

Jordan nodded, sensing Ash was being honest with her. She didn't know what to say. She wanted to be mad to learn Ash had known about the MS all this time and said nothing, but how could she be? But her knowing didn't change anything. Jordan would never allow anyone to pity her.

"I'm glad you know, Ash. Because now you understand why nothing can come of this."

"What? No, Jordan, I *don't* understand. Not at all. I understand you're scared, but I want to be there for you. I love you, and I want to spend my life with you, baby," Ash said as she got down on her knees between Jordan's legs, her hands resting on Jordan's thighs.

"And if I'm confined to a wheelchair next year? Or next month?"

"You could fall down a flight of stairs tomorrow, break your back, and be confined to a wheelchair. Or hell, I could. Nobody knows what the future holds, but I know this—I don't want to face a future without you. I let you go once, and it was the worst mistake of my life."

"If I can no longer be self-sufficient? If you have to feed me and change my diaper? Roll me over every so often so I don't get bedsores?"

"You know, you're the one here who has a preconceived idea that I would stay with you because I felt I had to. Because I might pity you." Ash squeezed her thigh to get her to look at her. She did feel sorry for her, but not because she had MS. It was because she'd managed to convince herself she had to face this alone. That no one could ever truly love her. "If it gets to that point, I wouldn't stay with you because I had to, I'd stay with you because I want to. Because I love you, and I would want to take care of you, just like I'd hope you would do for me if I ever needed it.

"But since you seem so determined to play the *if* game, let me ask you a question." She waited until Jordan gave a slight nod before continuing. "If I'd left my husband all those years ago and we'd built a life together, would you have left me when you were diagnosed? So you wouldn't have to wonder if I was only staying with you out of some sort of obligation?"

Jordan just stared at her, her eyes filling with tears. Ash wanted to hold her, but now wasn't the time. She'd said what she needed to say, and it was up to Jordan now. She stood and kissed Jordan on the cheek before walking to the door. Before leaving, she turned back to her.

"I don't want you to answer that now, but I want you to really think about it. If you can honestly answer yes, then I swear you'll never hear from me again. But if your answer is no, I'll be in Las Vegas. You know where to find me."

With that, she walked out, leaving Jordan crying. It was the hardest thing she'd ever done, but Jordan needed to do some soul-searching. That wasn't something she could do with Ash hanging around waiting and putting pressure on her to make a decision. Her own tears started to fall as she pulled out of the hotel parking lot and headed back home, wondering if she would ever see Jordan again.

CHAPTER THIRTY-ONE

Matt called Jordan to tell her they'd be allowed in to visit their mother in about an hour, so she quickly got dressed and headed back to the hospital. Since Ash had left over an hour earlier, Jordan hadn't been able to sleep. The question she'd asked kept replaying over and over again in her mind. It was a valid question, and even though she hadn't responded at the time, she knew what her answer was.

No.

No, she wouldn't have left her. What she wouldn't have given for Ash to be there by her side when she'd received her diagnosis. It had felt like someone punched her in the gut. After all the MRIs and brain scans and nerve tests, she'd never expected to be told she had MS. The doctor had mentioned it as a possibility early on, but her brain dismissed the notion. How could a few muscle spasms and some tingling in her arms and legs, and occasionally her scalp and face, be something as scary and unknown as MS?

She'd been told it was deemed an "orphan disease" because so few people in the world had it. Being classified that way also meant there wasn't much research into a cure because only about four hundred thousand people in the U.S. suffered from it.

She didn't remember driving herself back to the hospital, but she found herself exiting the elevator and walking to the waiting room to find Matt.

"Where's Ashley?"

"She went back home."

"What did you do?"

"Go to hell, Matt." Jordan was really not in the mood to put up with his know-it-all attitude. "Have you seen Mom yet?"

"I was just in there for a couple of minutes." He looked hurt by her insult, but Jordan couldn't muster enough energy to care at the moment. "She's still asking for you."

"Why?" They'd never gotten along very well. Before Jordan left for college, they both seemed to do everything they could to avoid each other. As a result, Matt usually ended up being their go-between. He shrugged, and Jordan knew it was because he was well aware of their difficult relationship.

Jordan paced, wondering what was so urgent she kept asking for her. Maybe she was adopted. God, that would be wonderful. But she looked at Matt and knew it wouldn't be wonderful. And the two of them looked so much alike. She reached out and grasped his hand for a moment before he told her what room she was in. She hugged him briefly then walked down the hall to find her.

She stopped just inside the door and was shocked at what she saw. Her mother looked so frail. So different than she had when Jordan was in Flagstaff less than a month ago for her birthday. She was hooked up to various machines that were all beeping out their own tunes. The doctor looked up and smiled as he waved her over.

"Mrs. Stryker, your daughter's here to see you," he told her. He replaced the chart at the foot of the bed and put a hand on Jordan's shoulder. "Keep it brief for now. She's still weak and sliding in and out of consciousness."

"Right," she said with a nod. She watched him leave the room and seriously considered following him, but then she heard her mother's voice, so quiet she almost thought she imagined it. She turned and saw her mother reaching out for her. Jordan took her hand and stepped up to the bed. She leaned in and pressed her lips to her cheek. "Hi, Mom."

"Jordan," she said with what looked to be a smile. Jordan wasn't completely sure about that though, since the right side of her face seemed to be paralyzed. "You came."

"Of course I did," she answered.

"Wasn't sure you would." She closed her eyes for so long Jordan wondered if she'd fallen asleep. Then she opened them again and looked right at her. "I was a horrible mother to you."

Jordan didn't know what to say. She wasn't going to argue the point because, well, it was true. She had no memory of either of her parents ever telling her they loved her. All they ever did was fight. Not just the two of them, but all four of them. Nothing she or Matt ever did was good enough for their parents. Of course, that changed as Matt got older and he apparently became the golden child.

Jordan stood there watching her mother, amazed at the recognition she could see in her eyes. She'd been surprised when Matt told her she'd asked for her, and even more surprised after she arrived to find out she was still asking for her. Her times of clarity never lasted this long. Maybe the stroke somehow managed to fix whatever wires had been loose in her brain.

"You always tried so hard to please your father and me, and we never appreciated it. I don't think either of us were ever cut out to be parents. I hope you know I've always loved you, in my own way. I just never knew how to show it. I'm so sorry."

"Mom, you should rest," Jordan said, trying to fight back the tears. "I love you too."

She was surprised to realize she meant it. She and Matt had always had food to eat and a roof over their heads, which was more than some kids had. She'd never seen it that way while living through it, but she could appreciate it now.

"I'm so proud of you. You're such a beautiful woman. I just want you to be happy. You deserve that, Jordan."

Jordan lost it then. She supposed it was as much of an acceptance of her homosexuality as she was ever going to get, and it was a hell of a lot more than she ever expected. Her mother squeezed her hand weakly and turned her head away from her. Jordan let go of her hand and leaned over to kiss her cheek again.

"Get well, Mom. We can spend a lot more time together when you get out of here."

She walked toward the door and was almost there when she heard the beeping of the heart monitor stutter and then it let out a shrill constant tone. Jordan turned to look at her mother. She had the presence of mind to step out of the way when the door crashed open and medical personnel hurried in to try to save her.

But it was too late. Jordan had the eerie feeling she'd only managed to hang on as long as she did so she could tell her those things. She felt a sense of peace knowing her mother's love for the first time in her life.

❖

"What's going on?" Matt asked as she walked down the hall toward him. She took his hand and led him to a chair.

"She's gone," was all she said.

"The doctor said—"

"She's gone, Matt. I'm sorry."

She expected him to cry. She expected him to fall to pieces. But he didn't. He stood and wrapped his arms around her, pulling her close. She hugged him back and they stayed there like that for a few moments.

"Did she tell you whatever it was she needed to tell you?"

"Yeah," she said as she pulled away with a nod. "Yeah, she did."

"Good. I'm going to wait here and take care of whatever I need to take care of. Why don't you go back to the hotel?"

"No, I'll wait with you."

They sat in a comfortable silence waiting for the doctor to come let them know their mother had passed away. After a few minutes, Matt turned toward her in his chair.

"What did she say?"

"She wanted to make sure I knew she loved me."

"Wow. Had she ever told you that before?"

"Not once." Jordan smiled and met his eyes. "It was nice to hear. She also told me I deserved to be happy."

"You do." Matt nodded and glanced down the hall toward her room. "Speaking of which, don't you need to go after Ashley?"

"It can wait until later." She rested her forearms on her knees and clasped her hands together. She really wanted to go after her, but this didn't seem like the right time. She needed to be with Matt for now.

"Like hell it can. At least call her. That way she won't spend the next few days wondering how you'll answer her question."

Jordan sat up straight and looked at him, not believing what she'd just heard. "Did she call you?"

"She came by here after she left you at the hotel to let me know what happened and to thank me for trying to help. You can be so damn stubborn sometimes, Jordan. Call the woman. Tell her you love her." Matt laughed as she sat there staring at him in disbelief. "And shut your mouth. You'll end up swallowing a fly."

Jordan waited a few more minutes until the doctor came by, then she left Matt to fill out the forms they needed and to make arrangements for their mother's body to be picked up by a funeral home. Jordan hurried outside to call Ash, hoping it wasn't too late.

"Jordan?" Ash said when she answered the phone.

"My mother died about thirty minutes ago."

"Oh, Jordan, I'm so sorry. Are you all right?"

"I'm okay." Jordan said, feeling at peace again. "Are you still driving?"

"Yes, I'm almost home."

"If I leave first thing in the morning, I can be there by noon." Jordan hesitated. When Ash didn't say anything, she started to worry. "That is if you want me there."

"That depends. Do you have an answer to my question?"

"Yes. No." Jordan sighed in frustration and raked her fingers through her hair. "I mean yes, I have an answer, and the answer is no. I would not have left you when I was diagnosed."

"So what does that mean for us?"

"I love you, Ash. I always have, and I always will. I want to give us a chance if you're still willing." Jordan held her breath as she waited for a response.

"Of course I am," Ash said, sounding relieved.

Jordan felt as though her heart might burst from joy. She didn't trust herself to talk at the moment because she was sure she was going to cry.

"Jordan, are you there?"

"I'll see you tomorrow?"

"Trixie and I will both be waiting for you."

Jordan disconnected and let out a relieved sigh.

"Everything okay?" Matt asked from behind her.

"Everything's perfect," she answered as she turned to face him. "You done here?"

"Yeah. Let's get something to eat."

CHAPTER THIRTY-TWO

Jordan made it to Henderson in just under three and a half hours. Her heart was pounding as she walked up to Ash's door at eleven thirty. She hesitated before she reached out and pushed the doorbell. She knew it was only a few seconds, but it seemed like an eternity before Ash opened the door and threw her arms around her, causing her to drop her duffel bag. Jordan didn't care though. Her arms went around Ash's waist and she held her close.

"I never want to spend another night without you," Ash said into her ear. "I hate not having you in the bed with me when I wake up."

"Me too," Jordan said. This feeling was more amazing than she thought it would be. The feeling of being loved by the person she loved. One-night stands had nothing on a committed relationship. At least that's what Jordan was hoping they were going to have. They'd need to have a talk about what was expected.

Ash pulled her inside and closed the doors from any prying neighbor's eyes. She motioned for Jordan to follow her to the kitchen, but Jordan had other ideas. She grasped her wrist and pulled her back to kiss her.

Ash's hands moved slowly up her arms until they reached her shoulders, then her arms went around Jordan's neck. Jordan's hands found the hem of Ash's T-shirt and started to pull it up over her head, but Ash broke their kiss and shook her head.

"There's plenty of time for that, lover," she said. Jordan grinned. "I'm guessing you left in such a hurry this morning you didn't eat anything, am I right?"

"Yes," she said sheepishly before following her into the kitchen. "But you never have any food here."

"After you called last night, before I came home, I went to the grocery store. There's so much food here, we probably wouldn't have to leave for days. Months, maybe." Ash looked proud of herself, and Jordan laughed.

Jordan came up behind her and slipped her arms around Ash's waist before pulling her back against her body and holding onto her tightly. Ash's hands covered hers and she leaned her head back against Jordan's shoulder.

"What if I want waffles and sausage?"

"Got it."

"Pancakes and bacon?"

"Check."

"A Southwestern omelet and buttermilk biscuits?"

"Yep, and I even got English muffins, ham, and everything you need to make hollandaise sauce so you can have eggs Benedict." Ash turned in her arms and kissed her lightly on the lips. "I'm pretty sure I thought of everything. Of course we'll be eating breakfast three times a day for the foreseeable future."

"That sounds wonderful to me." Jordan pressed her lips to Ash's jaw before moving her lips to her ear. "And you feel wonderful to me. Life is wonderful."

"We're really doing this, aren't we?"

"God, I hope so," Jordan said. She closed her eyes and breathed in the intoxicating scent that was uniquely Ash. The mixture of strawberry and sunshine with a hint of musk. "Let's go upstairs, baby."

"So, how is this going to work?"

Jordan took a step back and raised an eyebrow. "I'm sure you aren't referring to sex, because I happen to know for a fact you're quite good at it."

Ash swatted her playfully on the butt before heading to the living room.

"I've elected you head chef, but we need to talk before we can eat. There are some things we need to figure out."

"Okay, I sleep on the left side of the bed," Jordan said with a grin. They sat side by side on the couch and Ash leaned into her when she put an arm around her shoulders.

"I already know that. I was thinking about more serious things. Like do you want me to move to Philadelphia?"

The breath caught in Jordan's throat. Just the fact Ash would even suggest it spoke volumes about how much she loved her. She slowly ran her fingers through Ash's hair as she tried to gather her thoughts.

"It means the world to me for you to even consider that," she said after a moment. "But I don't want you to have to uproot your life again. I can move out here."

"Are you sure?" Ash pulled away and turned on the couch to face her. She held onto Jordan's hands as she spoke. "I would never ask you to do that."

"You didn't ask. I offered. And let's consider this rationally for a minute. You have a job you like," Jordan said, holding up a finger for each point she was making. "You have friends you consider family. I'd be closer to my brother. I proved I can hang with the big dogs in a poker tournament, and what better place for a poker player to live than Las Vegas? That's four things just off the top of my head in favor of us living here."

"And what about Philadelphia?"

"I can't think of a single reason to live there. If I hadn't transferred to the field office there I never would have moved to the East Coast."

"But you have a neurologist there. Are you sure you want to have to find a new one?"

"I don't care. They can transfer records. I'm sure there are some fine doctors out here. I assume Maria likes her doctor?"

"She can't say enough good things about him."

"Well then, there you go. I think it's settled." Trixie jumped up into her lap then and curled up into a ball. "Trixie doesn't want to move either, so if you don't mind having another person invade your space, I think we're going to live here."

"Cool," Ash said before turning serious. "I'm really sorry about your mom. I know you weren't close, but I'd think it would still have to be hard."

"It is a little tough," Jordan said. She told Ash the things her mother said to her before she died. It all seemed so surreal to Jordan that she might have actually had some semblance of a relationship with her mother if she'd been able to pull through.

"When do you have to go back to Arizona for the funeral? I might be able to get a couple days off to go with you if you want."

"Matt's having her cremated and decided against a funeral. Honestly, she didn't have any friends, so Matt and I would probably be the only people to show up. He's taking her ashes back to Phoenix with him."

Ash nodded. Jordan wasn't sure if she truly understood how difficult it would be for Matt if no one showed up to pay their respects. Jordan had been the one to suggest cremation, and he had readily agreed it would be best.

"I want us to be exclusive, Jordan," Ash said after a few moments. "Is that a problem?"

"I don't like to share, so it works for me." Jordan was relieved and she was sure it was obvious. Ash leaned forward and kissed her. She tried to pull away again but Jordan grasped her shoulders and held in place. "I love you, Ash, and I want to spend the rest of my life showing you every day exactly how much."

Jordan sunk into the cushions of the couch when Ash straddled her lap, causing Trixie to jump down and meow indignantly.

"You can start showing me now."

Jordan smiled. She was hungry, but food could wait until later.

About the Author

PJ Trebelhorn was born and raised in the greater metropolitan area of Portland, Oregon. Her love of sports—mainly baseball and ice hockey—was fueled in part by her father's interests. She likes to brag about the fact that her uncle managed the Milwaukee Brewers for five years, and the Chicago Cubs for one year.

PJ now resides in western New York with her wife, Cheryl, their four cats and one very neurotic dog. When not writing or reading, PJ enjoys watching movies, playing on the Playstation, and spending way too much time with stupid games on Facebook. She still roots for the Flyers, Phillies, and Eagles, even though she's now in Sabres and Bills territory.

Books Available from Bold Strokes Books

One Last Thing by Kim Baldwin & Xenia Alexiou. Blood is thicker than pride. The final book in the Elite Operative Series brings together foes, family, and friends to start a new order. (978-1-62639-230-4)

Songs Unfinished by Holly Stratimore. Two aspiring rock stars learn that falling in love while pursuing their dreams can be harmonious—if they can only keep their pasts from throwing them out of tune. (978-1-62639-231-1)

Beyond the Ridge by L.T. Marie. Will a contractor and a horse rancher overcome their family differences and find common ground to build a life together? (978-1-62639-232-8)

Swordfish by Andrea Bramhall. Four women battle the demons from their pasts. Will they learn to let go, or will happiness be forever beyond their grasp? (978-1-62639-233-5)

The Fiend Queen by Barbara Ann Wright. Princess Katya and her consort Starbride must turn evil against evil in order to banish Fiendish power from their kingdom, and only love will pull them back from the brink. (978-1-62639-234-2)

Up the Ante by PJ Trebelhorn. When Jordan Stryker and Ashley Noble meet again fifteen years after a short-lived affair, are either of them prepared to gamble on a chance at love? (978-1-62639-237-3)

Speakeasy by MJ Williamz. When mob leader Helen Byrne sets her sights on the girlfriend of Al Capone's right-hand man, passion and tempers flare on the streets of Chicago. (978-1-62639-238-0)

Venus in Love by Tina Michele. Morgan Blake can't afford any distractions and Ainsley Dencourt can't afford to lose control—but the beauty of life and art usually lies in the unpredictable strokes of the artist's brush. (978-1-62639-220-5)

Rules of Revenge by AJ Quinn. When a lethal operative on a collision course with her past agrees to help a CIA analyst on a critical assignment, the encounter proves explosive in ways neither woman anticipated. (978-1-62639-221-2)

The Romance Vote by Ali Vali. Chili Alexander is a sought-after campaign consultant who isn't prepared when her boss's daughter, Samantha Pellegrin, comes to work at the firm and shakes up Chili's life from the first day. (978-1-62639-222-9)

Advance: Exodus Book One by Gun Brooke. Admiral Dael Caydoc's mission to find a new homeworld for the Oconodian people is hazardous, but working with the infuriating Commander Aniwyn "Spinner" Seclan endangers her heart and soul. (978-1-62639-224-3)

UnCatholic Conduct by Stevie Mikayne. Jil Kidd goes undercover to investigate fraud at St. Marguerite's Catholic School, but life gets complicated when her student is killed—and she begins to fall for her prime target. (978-1-62639-304-2)

Season's Meetings by Amy Dunne. Catherine Birch reluctantly ventures on the festive road trip from hell with beautiful stranger Holly Daniels only to discover the road to true love has its own obstacles to maneuver. (978-1-62639-227-4)

Myth and Magic: Queer Fairy Tales edited by Radclyffe and Stacia Seaman. Myth, magic, and monsters—the stuff of childhood dreams (or nightmares) and adult fantasies. (978-1-62639-225-0)

Nine Nights on the Windy Tree by Martha Miller. Recovering drug addict, Bertha Brannon, is an attorney who is trying to stay clean when a murder sends her back to the bad end of town. (978-1-62639-179-6)

Driving Lessons by Annameekee Hesik. Dive into Abbey Brooks's sophomore year as she attempts to figure out the amazing, but sometimes complicated, life of a you-know-who girl at Gila High School. (978-1-62639-228-1)

Asher's Shot by Elizabeth Wheeler. Asher Price's candid photographs capture the truth, but when his success requires exposing an enemy, Asher discovers his only shot at happiness involves revealing secrets of his own. (978-1-62639-229-8)

Courtship by Carsen Taite. Love and justice—a lethal mix or a perfect match? (978-1-62639-210-6)

Against Doctor's Orders by Radclyffe. Corporate financier Presley Worth wants to shut down Argyle Community Hospital, but Dr. Harper Rivers will fight her every step of the way, if she can also fight their growing attraction. (978-1-62639-211-3)

A Spark of Heavenly Fire by Kathleen Knowles. Kerry and Beth are building their life together, but unexpected circumstances could destroy their happiness. (978-1-62639-212-0)

Never Too Late by Julie Blair. When Dr. Jamie Hammond is forced to hire a new office manager, she's shocked to come face to face with Carla Grant and memories from her past. (978-1-62639-213-7)

Widow by Martha Miller. Judge Bertha Brannon must solve the murder of her lover, a policewoman she thought she'd grow old with. As more bodies pile up, the murderer starts coming for her. (978-1-62639-214-4)

Twisted Echoes by Sheri Lewis Wohl. What's a woman to do when she realizes the voices in her head are real? (978-1-62639-215-1)

Criminal Gold by Ann Aptaker. Through a dangerous night in New York in 1949, Cantor Gold, dapper dyke-about-town, smuggler of fine art, is forced by a crime lord to be his instrument of vengeance. (978-1-62639-216-8)

The Melody of Light by M.L. Rice. After surviving abuse and loss, will Riley Gordon be able to navigate her first year of college and accept true love and family? (978-1-62639-219-9)

Because of You by Julie Cannon. What would you do for the woman you were forced to leave behind? (978-1-62639-199-4)

The Job by Jove Belle. Sera always dreamed that she would one day reunite with Tor. She just didn't think it would involve terrorists, firearms, and hostages. (978-1-62639-200-7)

Making Time by C.J. Harte. Two women going in different directions meet after fifteen years and struggle to reconnect in spite of the past that separated them. (978-1-62639-201-4)

Once The Clouds Have Gone by KE Payne. Overwhelmed by the dark clouds of her past, Tag Grainger is lost until the intriguing and spirited Freddie Metcalfe unexpectedly forces her to reevaluate her life. (978-1-62639-202-1)

The Acquittal by Anne Laughlin. Chicago private investigator Josie Harper searches for the real killer of a woman whose lover has been acquitted of the crime. (978-1-62639-203-8)

An American Queer: The Amazon Trail by Lee Lynch. Lee Lynch's heartening and heart-rending history of gay life from the turbulence of the late 1900s to the triumphs of the early 2000s are recorded in this selection of her columns. (978-1-62639-204-5)

Stick McLaughlin: The Prohibition Years by CF Frizzell. Corruption in 1918 cost Stick her lover, her freedom, and her identity, but a very special flapper and the family bond of her own gang could help win them back—even if it means outwitting the Boston Mob. (978-1-62639-205-2)

Edge of Awareness by C.A. Popovich. When Maria, a woman in the middle of her third divorce, meets Dana, an out lesbian, awareness of her feelings brings up reservations about the teachings of her church. (978-1-62639-188-8)

Taken by Storm by Kim Baldwin. Lives depend on two women when a train derails high in the remote Alps, but an unforgiving mountain, avalanches, crevasses, and other perils stand between them and safety. (978-1-62639-189-5)

The Common Thread by Jaime Maddox. Dr. Nicole Coussart's life is falling apart, but fortunately, DEA Attorney Rae Rhodes is there to pick up the pieces and help Nic put them back together. (978-1-62639-190-1)

Jolt by Kris Bryant. Mystery writer Bethany Lange wasn't prepared for the twisting emotions that left her breathless the moment she laid eyes on folk singer sensation Ali Hart. (978-1-62639-191-8)

Searching For Forever by Emily Smith. Dr. Natalie Jenner's life has always been about saving others, until young paramedic Charlie Thompson comes along and shows her maybe she's the one who needs saving. (978-1-62639-186-4)

A Queer Sort of Justice: Prison Tales Across Time by Rebecca S. Buck. When liberty is only a memory, and all seems lost, what freedoms and hopes can be found within us? (978-1-62639-195-6E)

Blue Water Dreams by Dena Hankins. Lania Marchiol keeps her wary sailor's gaze trained on the horizon until Oly Rassmussen, a wickedly handsome trans man, sends her trusty compass spinning off course. (978-1-62639-192-5)

Rest Home Runaways by Clifford Henderson. Baby boomer Morgan Ronzio's troubled marriage is the least of her worries when she gets the call that her addled, eighty-six-year-old, half-blind dad has escaped the rest home. (978-1-62639-169-7)

Charm City by Mason Dixon. Raq Overstreet's loyalty to her drug kingpin boss is put to the test when she begins to fall for Bathsheba Morris, the undercover cop assigned to bring him down. (978-1-62639-198-7)

Let the Lover Be by Sheree Greer. Kiana Lewis, a functional alcoholic on the verge of destruction, finally faces the demons of her past while finding love and earning redemption in New Orleans. (978-1-62639-077-5)

Blindsided by Karis Walsh. Blindsided by love, guide dog trainer Lenae McIntyre and media personality Cara Bradley learn to trust what they see with their hearts. (978-1-62639-078-2)

About Face by VK Powell. Forensic artist Macy Sheridan and Detective Leigh Monroe work on a case that has troubled them both for years, but they're hampered by the past and their unlikely yet undeniable attraction. (978-1-62639-079-9)

Blackstone by Shea Godfrey. For Darry and Jessa, their chance at a life of freedom is stolen by the arrival of war and an ancient prophecy that just might destroy their love. (978-1-62639-080-5)

Out of This World by Maggie Morton. Iris decided to cross an ocean to get over her ex. But instead, she ends up traveling much farther, all the way to another world. Once there, only a mysterious, sexy, and magical woman can help her return home. (978-1-62639-083-6)